MAGNOLIA

FIRST OF A DUET

WILLOW WINTERS

WALL STREET JOURNAL & USA TODAY BESTSELLING AUTHOR

From USA Today bestselling author Willow Winters comes a steamy, second chance romance.

He tasted like tequila and the fake name I gave him was Rose.

Four years ago, I decided to get over one man by getting under another. It was supposed to be a single night and nothing more.

I found my handsome stranger with a shot glass at the end of the bar, along with a charming but devilish smile. The desire that filled his eyes the second they landed on me ignited a spark inside me, instant and hot. He was perfect and everything I didn't know I needed. That one night may have ended too soon, but I left with much more than a memory.

Four years later, and with a three-year-old in tow, I'm back home in the quiet little town I grew up in. As the man I still dream about stares at me from across the street, the flash of recognition and the heat in his gaze are unmistakable. The chemistry between us is still there, even after all these years.

I just hope the secrets and regrets don't destroy our second chance before it's even begun.

TEQUILA ROSE

CHAPTER 1

MAGNOLIA

FOUR YEARS AGO...

COLLEGE CAMPUS ON THE EAST COAST

I lie to myself. That's what a person does when they're hurt. They say they're not hurt at all.

"I'm fine ... and Robert can go fuck himself." The additional statement is an extra special truth to make the lie okay. I'm dead set on the words coming out of my mouth even though I'm alone in my apartment with no one here to listen to my declaration. The ball of anxiousness and betrayal in my throat lodges itself deep at the mere mention of his name. Funny enough, every gulp of Sweet Red I take seems to ease that cruel combo down and shrink it so I can swallow the bitter breakup.

Wine and cupcakes. That's what I've been working with tonight. I could eat a dozen cupcakes right now, but I only had two left over ... and even the remnants of the frosting on their containers is gone. So now I'm down to just wine.

Alcohol, sweets and trash TV is supposed to be how a girl deals with a breakup, right?

I'm trying my darnedest to take all this in stride, but it freaking hurts. I've never been with anyone else. I've never loved anyone else. I don't even know how to handle a "breakup." If I can even call it that. He dumped me. Plain and simple. My high school sweetheart, the man I've been with for five years dumped me, and he did it over a freaking phone call.

Tears prick the back of my eyes remembering how we just slept together when I was home last week and how adamantly I believed the words that came out of his mouth when he told me he loved me. I feel so stupid for believing him. I'm a fool for having no idea that this was going to happen.

I need more cupcakes. Shoot, maybe I should buy a full-blown cake at this point.

I pick up the half-empty bottle of red wine and pour another helping into the pale pink mug. You can achieve any goal you can dream is printed on the other side of it in a silver, feminine script. My goal right now: get wasted. And yes, I can achieve it. One point for me.

I don't own shot glasses, but a bottle of citrus vodka is

next. Not having wineglasses didn't hinder the wine, so why should a lack of shot glasses hinder the vodka? Two weeks ago, when I turned twenty-one and partied in my hometown to celebrate the last year I'd have away at college, my best friend, Renee, poured all the shots that night and left me the bottle. She's a bartender back at home. Moving away from one of South Carolina's coastal Sea Islands was insane for me to do in Renee's eyes. She's never had any intention of leaving. Not for college, not for anything. She loves the boating life and sea breeze. As do my other friends.

Maybe that's why Robert ended it. This long-distance relationship is too much all of a sudden. That doesn't make sense, though. Maybe it was the long distance that kept him from severing the relationship. In less than a year, I'll be back in our small town and it wouldn't be a long-distance relationship anymore. Maybe he could deal with me far away, but in reality he didn't want me anymore. I just don't understand. Ugh, that hurts, that deep-seated insecurity that just burrowed into the pit of my stomach.

"Another gulp it is," I joke bitterly and toss the mug back.

I'll be fine. I know I will.

In fact, I'll be better than fine.

I have everything going for me and now I'm free ... and Robert can go fuck himself. I clink my empty mug with an imaginary one in front of me. It takes a half second for me to break into a grin and laugh at just how pathetic this is.

The clank of the mug hitting my coffee table makes me wince and then a small chuckle leaves me as my shoulders hunch. "Oops."

With my pointer tapping the soft tip of my nose, I take a look around my trashed apartment. After our very short-lived phone call this afternoon where he took all of ten minutes to tell me it was over, barely letting me get a word in, I threw out everything that reminded me of my POS ex. Which didn't leave me with much. There are lots of soft blues and pops of lavender and pink in the décor that remains. Especially in the mugs, the throw pillows and blankets. Nearly all of my pictures are gone ... I shouldn't have thrown away those frames.

A whitewashed frame holding an eight-by-ten of Renee, Sharon, Autumn and me takes up the full shelf to the right of the TV. The rest of the shelving unit no longer exists.

Dammit.

Robert and I promised each other under our special angel oak tree back home that we would be together forever. No, it wasn't a proposal, but it was a promise.

Not one he meant to keep, apparently.

We made that promise when we were still kids, but it meant something to me.

The sofa groans as I lean back into it, pulling my knees into my chest. I had no idea he didn't love me anymore. That's what is really getting to me. It's like whiplash. We were just together, laughing, holding each other's hands. He kissed my knuckles in front of all of our friends. Even his smile ...

I can't. Blinking rapidly, I stand up abruptly and force those memories out of my head. With the press of the clicker, music videos take over the screen—sorry, housewives—and I turn up the volume to something that sounds like a mix of country and pop.

The lyrics elude me, but I like the beat. It guides me to my closet and that's when I hear the chorus and recognize the song.

Even though my face is blotchy from crying, makeup will cover it.

I refuse to wallow in my living room and pity myself.

Renee told me most men kiss the same but then there are others who are different.

I've only kissed one man my whole life. Tonight, I'm going to find out if he's one of the ones who kisses the same. Or if his was different.

Pausing my motions as I pull a red chiffon shift dress out of the closet, I realize that means I'd have to kiss more than one man. Because what if they are different? If two kisses are different, the one from some random guy tonight compared to the ones Rob gave me ... then how would I know which guy gave the same type of kiss that every other guy gives?

A groan slips from my lips as I pull the dress off the hanger completely and then rub a hand down my face.

That's too complicated. I'll just call it what it is. Revenge sex, a rebound, a fling. That's what I want tonight. And I aim to get it. My father may think I'm a Southern belle, but a scorned woman is a scorned woman and that's just what I am.

Cupcakes and alcohol at eleven at night can't steer me wrong, right?

CHAPTER 2

MAGNOLIA

I'm not second-guessing the red dress; red is a confident color, and a color to wear for good luck, at that. With my blond wavy hair only slightly brushed so it's a bit wild, the simple dress makes me look a bit more refined. But I'm starting to question what I was thinking when I picked out these heels. I try not to wince or make it too noticeable as I carefully slip the right one off just a little. Just a teeny tiny bit for some relief. I'm seated at the bar so I don't think a soul notices.

The Louis Vuittons were a birthday gift from my dad. They're expensive, utterly gorgeous, and brand new, ergo not broken in. My feet are killing me after walking from my apartment complex to Main Street where the string of bars was waiting for me. It's only a mile, and in flip-flops or sneakers it's an easy walk. Nice even. But in these heels ... My bottom lip drops just slightly, letting a low hiss slip out as the mix of agony and relief swirl and hit me harder than the liquor has all night.

Mistake number one tonight: these heels.

I'll definitely be taking an Uber home.

"What'll it be?" the bartender asks me, and I peek up at him. I lost a lot of my courage on the way down here. The tipsiness is waning far too quickly. I picked the Blue Room because a friend from class, Michelle, usually hangs out here. She's nowhere in sight, though.

"My friend gets a drink here ... something like Cherry ..." I let my voice trail off and hope he knows what I'm talking about. The handsome man has to be in his late thirties judging by the faint wrinkles around his brown eyes. His hair, a little longer than I prefer in men, is swept back and the color matches his black tie. The Blue Room has a fabulous dress code for their employees, in my opinion. It's all white dresses just above knee length for the women, and crisp white dress shirts rolled up to the elbows for the men. With the skinny tie he's wearing, I have to admit it's a sleek, sexy look that matches the décor in this place. It's a nod at a speakeasy, I think.

"It's called Cherry something," I say and chew my lip, trying to remember the name.

Michelle ordered a round when I got back from my

birthday celebration in Beaufort. "It's delicious but I don't remember the name," I add when he gives me a look like he has no idea what I'm talking about.

Shoot.

"Berry Drop?" a bartender a few feet away chimes in. He's the same height, but a smaller build than the man standing on the other side of the polished wooden counter in front of me.

"Gotcha," my bartender says and nods then immediately goes for a cup of ice, making the drink without waiting for me to acknowledge the name.

"It is delicious," he adds when he finally looks at me, grabbing two liquor bottles, plus a third.

The whole darn thing looks like it's made of alcohol. There's some kind of rule about mixing alcohols, but I'm pretty sure those rules don't count when it comes to breakups.

I watch him add a scoop of fresh berries into the silver shaker and note how much I love this campus, this bar and the East Coast.

My dad didn't understand why I wanted to leave South Carolina. None of my friends got it either. University of Delaware is a party school and I came here with undecided as my degree of choice.

It was either that or art history, which my father forbade. It wasn't a serious enough path, according to him. I still haven't had the balls to tell him that it's what my degree will be in. Maybe I'll get lucky and he'll be too busy with schmoozing and planning meetings to pay my degree any mind.

The tall cylindrical glass clanks in front of me, beads of condensation already rolling down its cool sides. "Berry Drop," the bartender announces proudly and nods at me to have a sip. Resting his clasped hands in front of him, he waits as I take a sip.

The smile that comes to my lips is immediate and apparently contagious, because he smiles too, claps once in victory, then moves to the end of the crowded bar.

I'm all the way at the other end in the corner, where I can see everyone else. There's an empty stool next to me, but the rest of the place is buzzing with life.

I keep drinking, sucking down the delicious cocktail as I people watch. It seems to be mostly groups of men and women at the tables. The floor is packed with bodies, though, couples dancing and laughing. I'm sure some don't even know each other; they're simply here doing what I'm doing: looking for someone to get into trouble with.

Maybe just to flirt, to feel someone against their skin. Maybe to share a kiss or two. I suck on the straw and air slips in, making that familiar white noise sound. I have to shake the cup to move some of the ice out of the way, frowning as I realize I've already gone through my drink in a matter of minutes ...

It's not that there wasn't enough in the glass. It's that it was simply that easy to drink it down.

"You need another?" a friendly masculine voice, not the

professional one of the bartender, asks from my right. Just hearing that deep baritone stirs up jitters in my stomach. I can feel his presence before I see him. He's tall, much taller than I am, which is more than obvious when he sits down on the stool next to me and I have to crane my neck to look up at him.

This place has sleek, minimalistic décor; the seat beneath this man isn't enough for him. It's too simple for a man with obvious rough edges. His shirt clings to his broad shoulders as he leans against the bar, folding his arms so the muscles in his forearms coil all the way up to his biceps.

His charming smile only adds to the draw he has. The air bends around him, and every woman in this place is eyeing him up. If Man Candy Mondays had a mascot, this man would be it.

It takes him smirking at me, letting out a gruff sound of humor from between his perfectly white teeth, for me to realize I haven't answered him.

I feel dizzy, warm and fuzzy. It's the drink, I tell myself. Slipping the straw back into my mouth and finishing off the last tiny bit, I add, I'm a bad liar.

"Yes please, if you're offering," I say as seductively as I can and my legs sway a little from side to side, my nerves betraying me as the words slip out. In my long walk down here, I forgot one very important thing ... It's been five years since I've flirted with anyone. I may be a touch rusty.

He leans back, giving me a good view of his broad chest

which looks like it's been carved from marble.

In dark jeans and a thin black T-shirt, he looks blue collar through and through. Someone who works with his hands and all that physical labor only makes him that much sexier.

Mistake number two: accepting a drink from this man.

He's too good looking. Too charming. Too practiced at this game of "can I buy you a drink?" flirtation.

"You go here?" I ask to make small talk as he lifts his hand to get the attention of the bartender, busy making another drink. The bartender nods after my new company gives him the order: another for her, and an IPA, tall.

"No," he says with a shake of his head and turns his full attention to me. "You?"

The drink appears in front of me before I know it. And with my pointer finger and thumb keeping the straw steady, I do my best to keep up conversation while reminding myself that I'm supposed to be flirting.

"Yup, art history major."

"Oh yeah? What are you going to do with that?" he asks, lifting the beer to his sculpted lips. He never takes his eyes off of me. I like it. I crave his attention more than I should.

I shrug as if I don't have it all planned out. Because I don't, not anymore. Robert's family owns a museum just outside of town and I always thought I'd work there. So much for that idea. I'll be looking at any other museum in the country than the one with his family's name on it.

The thought is unwelcome and a new sense of loss washes over me. I take a good long sip before picking out a blueberry to suck on.

"You live around here then?" I ask, desperate to change subjects.

"Visiting a friend."

I glance behind him and then turn to get a better view of the place. "Where is he?" I presume his friend is male and then correct myself, adding, "Or she?"

He shakes his head once, placing both his hands on the bar and tapping his thumbs like they're drumming to the music. "No she."

The answer warms me and I have to put my drink down for a moment before I find this one gone too quickly as well.

"He is busy tonight and left me to look after his place while he's out of town."

"So you're house-sitting?" I ask and finally get a good look at his eyes. They're baby blue, such a pale shade. It's not fair how God made some people roam this earth looking like sex on a stick.

"Yeah, I've got the time and he had to head out on short notice."

"Work let you off without a problem?" I say, wondering what he does for a living.

"I work for myself. So yeah."

"Entrepreneur?" I ask to pry further, wondering if he's

lying and this is a pickup routine he does. If it is, it's working.

I've never thought of myself as horny. Especially since I've been in a long-distance relationship for three years and going without sex never bothered me. Sitting next to Mr. Right Now, though ... I am not too far away from being all-out needy.

The conversation is easy and flows. Every time I laugh, my knees sway a little too much to the right and brush against him. One time his hand grazes them and with the light touch I can feel those sparks other people talk about.

Time passes, and I feel all sorts of things I'm not sure I've ever felt before. It's all so new and I wonder if this is what Sharon refers to when she talks about "first flirt jitters."

"You have an accent," he says and I laugh at the comment, a little too loud. Rolling my eyes, I set down the shot glass, our second together, on the polished bar and look at it rather than those piercing blue eyes I can feel drifting down the crook of my neck.

I wonder if he's thinking about kissing me there. With his rough stubble, I imagine it would feel coarse and scratch my neck. Heat simmers along my skin, but it's even hotter between my thighs. I wonder for a moment what it would be like to feel his stubble down there. I want to feel that. I want to feel what that's like.

Am I really going to do it? I think as the shots finally seem to hit my brain, making me a little more blurred than fuzzy.

"I think I've had enough," I say, my voice full of humor and I know the smile is still present on my face. I can feel one plastered there. I'm a chicken. I've always been a little scaredy-cat.

"What's wrong?" he asks and he reaches out to help me get off the barstool. I'm a little too short and grateful for the help. But the second his skin touches mine, electricity ignites, every nerve ending coming alive.

The barstool scrapes against the ground as I get up, trying to stand on my own.

My feet slip back into my heels and I stumble, caught off guard by the slight hint of pain. With a yelp from my lips, my hand reaches out to grab on to something, anything.

I didn't need to, because he's quick to wrap his own strong arm around my back. He's all hard muscle, coiled around me tight. Being this close to him, his masculine scent hits me suddenly. It's like a cool breeze across the sea. Fresh with a hint of rain coming. He smells like home.

I'm too busy getting lost in him to realize my hand is far too close to his ... downstairs.

"Oh!" I jump back, and he eases his grip on me immediately. My grimace fades when humor glints in his gorgeous eyes. "Sorry," I whisper. The wince is from embarrassment, not from my shoes this time.

"You all right?" he asks, sitting back in his seat but not taking his gaze off me. The suggestion of laughter still lingers on his lips, but he eyes me with concern.

"I had a little before I got here," I tell him with a nod. "You know, alcohol."

"Uh-huh," he says and smirks at me.

"So I'm just feeling a little tipsy."

"You need a glass of water."

"I just want to go for a second."

"Running away, then?" he asks and I gawk at him.

Shaking my head, I deny it and say, "I'm not running away." Although that's exactly what I was going to do. I lie when I add, "I'm just going to the restroom to wash my hands."

"To wash your hands?"

"It's the polite thing to say." I lower my voice. "Would you rather I tell you I have to pee?"

His laugh is unexpected. It's louder than the chuckles before, genuine and everything I want to hear from those lips right now. It's deep and the cadence is as rough as the calluses on his hands.

"You're real cute," he tells me, his smile reaching his eyes. "Can I at least have your name?"

Mags. My name is there on the tip of my tongue. But that's what Robert called me.

I don't want to be Magnolia.

Tonight, I want to be a rose. Beautiful and delicate, but covered in thorns. You can't fuck with a rose.

"Rose," I say, lying for the second time tonight. In a

matter of five minutes, I've already lied to this man twice. Once about running away, and now about my name. I'm not proud of that, but the way he murmurs Rose like he's tasting it on his tongue, makes me feel just about okay with lying.

Maybe even good. That bit of heat from before ripples through me, and the ease that washes away the panic that hit me a moment ago, that definitely feels better than good.

"And you?" I ask and he simply stares at me. For one long second and then another. "Your name?" I add, thinking maybe I didn't make sense.

His tongue clicks against the roof of his mouth, drawing attention to both his strong jawline and his gorgeous lips. Especially the bottom one. My gaze stays there another second before I realize I'm waiting on him to give me his name.

"Why don't you head to the bathroom, or wherever you're going," he says confidently. "I'll tell you when you get back."

He flashes me a wink with an asymmetrical grin playing at his lips, right before turning back to the bar. The music and chatter are so loud around me that I can't hear what he tells the bartender.

It doesn't matter, though. The bathroom is my refuge. Every step I take to get there, every second I spend in the small line before I can snag a stall, I think about whether or not I'm actually going back to the bar.

Apparently, I really did have to pee.

It's not until I think about what I'd do if I did go home

that I make my decision. I've cried enough already today. I'm not going home to hug my pillow and feel that loneliness again. A little touch-up of powder and gloss is all I need. My cheeks are a bit flushed, but hey, how could they not be after sitting next to that man?

Mistake number three: going back to the bar.

The third time is the charm, isn't it?

"You came back," Mr. Hot Stuff comments and it forces a blush to heat my cheeks.

Sliding back onto the barstool and getting myself situated, I let out a huff of protest. "I said I would."

"Brody," he says and the one word finally hits me. Brody. The sex god has a name.

"I've never met a Brody before," I say absently. I thought maybe, while I was in the bathroom, that he wasn't as good looking as I imagined him to be. Beer goggles had taken effect or something. But looking at him from his profile to his broad shoulders, no one could ever deny Brody is a good-looking man.

"Nice to meet you, Rose." The moment he says my fake name, a basket hits the bar, stealing my attention. It's hot and filled with slices of fried pickles. My mouth waters instantaneously. My favorite. Some people have a sweet tooth; I've got a salt tooth.

"And a water," the bartender says, placing a tall, clear glass in front of me.

"Oh, I didn't order this," I say to correct him, although I will definitely be ordering fried pickles the moment he takes them away.

"I think you might need them," Brody tells me, leaning in close. I get another whiff of him, but it's too short lived as he pulls away. "You've got to share the pickles, though. They're my favorite."

"Mine too," I say, pushing the basket so it's between the both of us instead of in front of my lonesome seat. "Whenever they're on a menu, I always get them."

I pop the first one into my mouth and bite down, but immediately my mouth makes an O and I breathe out. "They're hot," I comment around the pickle and cover my mouth with both hands. The steam blows against them.

I feel like such a mess and foolish.

Brody's chuckle eases me, though. I could get used to a laugh like that and the way it lights me up is like something I haven't felt before.

Maybe it's just because I haven't flirted in so long. That has to be why I feel all these butterflies.

I can't even remember the last time I had fun like this.

We stay until "Closing Time" plays on the speakers and they turn the lights on full blast in the bar, ushering us out. By that point, everything is a blur. It all happens so fast but it's seemingly so right.

It turns out Brody's a gentleman, waiting with me for my

Uber to come. It's colder than it was when I came down here and he gives me his jacket. As he's doing it, I get up on my tiptoes and steal a kiss. Surprise lights inside of me that I did it. Then other feelings spread through me.

My kiss may have been short and sweet but the one Brody gives me in return, with his hand on my chin and his scent and warmth wrapping around me, is anything but short. It's also far more sinful than sweet.

Renee was right about the kiss. Some men do kiss in a way that's different. Searing. I don't need to kiss another man in my life to know that this one isn't like any of the rest.

I knew I shouldn't have gone home with him but I did anyway, having the Uber take us to his friend's place instead of mine.

I didn't pay attention to where we were going and where he was taking me. I was too busy with my lips pressed to his while my eyes were closed.

I was still at his friend's place, contemplating sneaking out and accepting the walk of shame with my head held high when my phone rang far too early the next morning. I could still feel him and the dull ache of a good night when I answered the call with a whisper in his bathroom.

Everything changed in that moment.

I snuck out after crying silently on the floor of his bathroom, not letting him see what a wreck I was after the call.

The one-night stand I had was my first and last.

Because that morning, my life changed forever ... in more than one way.

CHAPTER 3

MAGNOLIA

PRESENT DAY IN BEAUFORT, SOUTH CAROLINA

Bridget's curls bounce like they have a mind of their own. I don't know where she gets the light brunette color from, but those curls are all mine.

She doesn't even look back to say goodbye to me; all I can see is a head of golden curls as she races to sit down in the circle on the bright blue rug. I think taking her to the library for weekly readings was exactly what she needed to transition to daycare. She knows all the little songs by heart and plops down next to Sandra's little ones like she belongs right there. Autumn told me it would help the shift in her routine and she was so right.

And to think I thought today would be hard on Bridget

and not me. A long, slow breath leaves me, my cheeks puffed as I wave goodbye to Trent, the owner. I grew up next to him and his mom ran this daycare before he did.

"It'll be good for her," she says and Renee doesn't try to hide the amusement in her voice in the least as she pushes open the front door. A little beep went off just before and I turn to look over my shoulder to say goodbye again.

"I know, knock it off," I say then hip bump her as our heels click on the sidewalk. It's only 9:00 a.m. and we're late for Bridget's first day here, but the court hearing was earlier. Everyone in town knows that. And court took precedent. Thank goodness Renee loves watching Bridget in the morning. I know Autumn or Sharon would help out with Bridget if they could, but their mornings on a good day are even more hectic than mine was today.

"Let's grab drinks tonight and celebrate this mess being over," Renee says, taking the lead with her suggestion as she opens her driver side door and I climb into the passenger seat.

I feel drained and emotional and I wish I had half the energy and confidence Renee has right now.

The sound of her keys clanging together isn't followed with the start of the engine. It's quiet, too quiet, and I tilt my head, leaning it back against the seat to see her big hazel eyes staring back at me.

"Wine Down Wednesday with the girls?" I ask but she shakes her head.

"Something tonight."

"I don't know about tonight …" I want to crawl in bed and sleep for a decade after what I just went through. She must read my thoughts in my expression.

"Maggie, it's done and over with. You can breathe now."

I make a show of puffing up my cheeks again and blowing out an annoyingly long breath just for her. I would have kept going but she laughs and that makes me laugh.

"That's better," she says and gives me a shit-eating grin.

"You know I love you, right?"

She hesitates to back out of the parking space after starting the car, and the music from the radio fills the small space. I have to reach over to turn it down before I add, "I couldn't do this without you."

Renee swipes a wild strand of her auburn hair out of her face then says, "Yes you could. And I love you too."

I roll my eyes at her nonchalance and buckle up for whatever she has planned.

I'm not working today since it's Bridge's first day at daycare. Although I told my boss it's because of the court hearing.

"She got nothing." Renee places a singsong cadence on the last word.

"She didn't deserve anything," I say and stare straight ahead as we pass Main Street. The bakery's sign is getting a fresh coat of bright white paint around the script letters that read Melissa's Sweets.

I roll down the window and the faint smell of fresh mulch and spring flowers fills my lungs. Resting against the seat, I take in all the small-town shops that have been here since I was a child. From way back when my mother was still alive and my father still pretended to be a good man.

"I'm sorry you had to go through it all," Renee says and this time she sounds serious.

My throat's tight as I smile at her and give a little nod. "It's done now."

"Still ..." she trails off then huffs, and the wind from her own rolled-down window blows back her hair. "To go through the scandal, the breakup, your dad dying. All at once and not getting closure for three years." She shakes her head slightly.

"A small sum of money isn't closure," I say, correcting her. "I lost my dad a long time ago. Four freaking years. The scandal isn't mine, even if everyone acts like it is."

"He tainted your name. Williamson used to hold a certain regard in this town. Your family was a good family with a trusted name." Even though the car comes to a halt at the stop sign, she keeps talking.

She's not saying anything I don't know but instead of looking at her as she rants, I watch Mr. Henderson tend to his garden in his front yard.

"Your father destroyed your family name, left you with nothing after embezzling and stealing from practically every family in this town. Nothing but a money-hungry ho who fought you for four years over the pennies he left behind."

The way she says the last sentence under her breath makes me chuckle. It's been more than three years, the settlement is final and now I can finally breathe. I just need to shake off all this bad energy.

"And the bastard had the nerve to die of a heart attack when it all broke."

My father was an asshole for what he did, but I still hate that he died so suddenly. I hate that I have no family. Especially in a small town like this. Tears prick, but I keep them back.

"I'm sorry, Mags." Renee's no-nonsense attitude is what I need ninety-nine percent of the time. Maybe today I should take some time alone, though.

"Today's just an emotional day," I say, giving her the lame excuse and dabbing under my eyes as we move forward. I focus on the scenery of the town I grew up in as it passes us by. Beaufort is a beautifully maintained small town with Southern charm.

Anyone who comes here for a visit would fall in love.

They don't see that it's filled with old secrets. Grudges passed down from generations long past. And judgment from literally everyone. This town talks and four years ago, the name Williamson became synonymous with scandal.

I was a debutante and heir to an enterprise my father built. In one night, I became a pariah. Add in the pregnancy conception that night too and well, no one wanted a thing to do with me.

I had debt I couldn't cover. An education I couldn't continue with ... having the rug ripped out from under me didn't exactly make perfect sense at the age of twenty-one.

"I'm happy I have you and Robert." I come to the conclusion at the same time I speak the words. I have my two other girlfriends too, but as we've gotten older, our time together is less and less. Four years ago, when shit hit the fan, I didn't want to be around anyone. Renee insisted on helping me, and Robert, much to my surprise, did too. I didn't realize how much I needed them to get through it all. I don't know how I would have survived without them.

Renee's brow raises at "Robert," but she bites her tongue.

"You know I couldn't have stayed here if he hadn't helped me." She knows that's true. Not a single soul who was capable of helping offered me any assistance. Renee is my best friend, but she didn't know a single thing about the charges and how the legalities would play out, let alone have the money to pay for everything up front. Robert did, using his local family connections, and he stood by me when no one else with his background would.

The town whispers that he still loves me. They think I broke up with him when I found out I got pregnant by someone I cheated on him with. Inwardly, I roll my eyes. They have no idea what the truth is, but I let them talk. I wouldn't tarnish Robert's name when he's the only one who protected me and provided for me financially, emotionally ... and in other ways too.

"He stood by you in one way and threw you under the bus in another."

"Because he didn't want to date me anymore?" My voice is filled with ridicule.

Renee remains silent. She knows what happened when most people here don't.

"Thank you for not judging me," I say softly, not wanting to fight. Especially not over Robert. If Renee is known for anything, it's the fact that she can hold a grudge like no other.

"I would never judge you. Never, Mags. Never. You have to do what's right for you," she says, her tone adamant as we pull up to my townhouse. "Even if you are a complete disgrace to your Southern heritage," she says, mocking Robert's mother's accent.

Everyone else I give a pass to because that's just how this town is. That woman, though, is a bitch with a stick up her ass. I don't even like to cuss, but she gets two of those words in her description in my thoughts.

The car slows to a stop in front of my door.

"I'll pick you up at eight?" she suggests and I relent to the idea of having a few drinks to celebrate.

"Yeah. Eight works," I answer and mindlessly go over the schedule I have for today. Opening my car door, I think out loud and say, "Miss Terbont will be here then. Although you know she's usually ten minutes late."

Renee grins wide and says, "That works for me. I can have a quick tea party with my little Bridgey."

"Perfect," I say and shut the door after adding, "See you tonight, love."

Renee blows a kiss to me and I watch her drive off before finding the key to my front door.

I don't need it, though, since Robert's standing on my porch with a handsome smile on his face.

"Robert." I greet him warmly and can't help that I smile when I see the way he looks at me. Once you have love for someone, I think it's always there. Either that or hate, and I could never hate him.

He's always in dress pants and a tie. The one he's wearing right now is my favorite. The deep navy blue fabric matches his eyes and makes them pop. With a clean-shaven face showing off his angular jaw and his hair cut short, but a little longer on top, he is the epitome of a Southern gentleman. A good ole boy with dirty blond hair and a twinkle in his eyes.

"Told you that you'd win," he says with a slightly cocky undertone and then he reaches out for me. His strong arms open wide and I don't hesitate to fall into him. He lets out a rough groan of victory as he picks me up off my feet.

I don't mean to squeal but it's my instinct.

I'm still laughing when he sets me down on my feet, my

heels clicking and then I open the door.

Tossing the keys on the kitchen counter and flicking the lights on, I don't bother asking him to come in. He owns the place, after all.

It's modest but with updated appliances and has everything Bridget and I could need or want. My purse drops to the rustic front table that matches the rest of the place. The pops of teal and yellow throughout keep it happy and bright. It's a home. Robert helped me build a home for my little girl and I don't think Renee can understand that.

"You want to celebrate?" he asks as he kicks the door shut behind him. Even after everything we've been through, he still manages to ignite desire inside of me. He's already working on loosening the knot of his tie. The poor guy is about to have blue balls.

"I can't," I tell him, giving him a small pout to mirror the one that immediately appears on his face.

"Should I come by later tonight?"

"I'm going out with Renee," I answer him as I watch him struggle to knot the tie again.

He may be twenty-five, but he looks older, more dignified. We've both gone through some rough moments in our lives; I imagine that's what they do to people. They age them.

Still ... he's charming, sweet, comes from money and has a bright future in politics. He shouldn't be with me. Both of us know it, yet here we are. It would have been so easy for him to walk away.

"After, then?" he asks, lifting up his collar and watching his movements in the small mirror in the foyer while he fiddles with the tie.

"After what?" My wandering thoughts are ripped back to the present.

"Should I come by tonight, after you celebrate with your friends?"

"Do you collect rent from all your tenants that late at night?" I tease him and then step in between him and the small table, helping him adjust his tie again. The expensive silk slides easily for me. I've done this so many times. His hands land protectively on my hips and I hate how much it soothes the little broken pieces inside me.

I've relied on a man who keeps me a secret. A dirty little secret of being a kept woman. I have money to pay rent, but he refuses to take it. At first he said he was just helping out a friend. I needed more than a friend, though. Losing my house, my inheritance being stalled because of my father's entitled girlfriend, and needing to figure out how I was going to raise a child on my own, was almost too much for me to deal with. When it all kept piling up, one thing on top of another, I needed far more than a friend to help me handle the curveballs life kept throwing at me.

Robert gave me what I needed. Even if it was wrong in some ways.

He isn't my boyfriend and he'll never be my husband. Yet I let him come and go as he pleases. More than that, I seek refuge in our messed-up relationship.

I pat his chest when the tie is firmly where it should be, but he doesn't move his hands from my waist.

"I'm happy it's over, Mags," he whispers deep and rough, bending down to kiss the tip of my nose. It's instinct to lean into him and he wraps his arms around me like a comforting blanket.

"Me too," I murmur into his firm chest.

"Shit, I can't come tonight," he says. His acknowledgment has him taking a step back and I right myself. Pinching the bridge of his nose, he mutters, "I have that dinner with the governor."

Two years ago, at the start of his political track he would have been eager and excited for the dinner. Now he's a pro and all the meetings and fundraisers blur together.

Politics is why he could never be with a woman like me. How could he ever win an election in the South, marrying a "disgraced" woman like me? I roll my eyes at the thought. It's not like I'm looking for anything anyway. I haven't since the moment my life fell apart, followed by my little baby girl falling into my lap.

"I hope you have some pretty little arm candy to accompany you to this one," I say to rib him a little, giving him my back as I slip off my heels.

He doesn't answer even though it's just a joke. It gets to him sometimes, the fact that we're quiet about all this between us. I'm grateful for the relationship. Without him, I don't know how I would have navigated all the lawyers and financial troubles. Let alone cope with life in general.

I will always love Robert for being there for me. Even if I'm nothing more than his little secret.

I give him a peck on the lips, grabbing ahold of his shoulders. "Have fun tonight; I'll see you tomorrow."

CHAPTER 4

BRODY

"It's good, isn't it?" Griffin's question comes with the hollow thunk of his empty glass hitting the bar-height table in the back corner of the brewery. "The best recipe yet." He double taps the bottom of his tasting glass after throwing back the small bit of what was left in it.

The sweet taste of hops is fresh and, more importantly, smooth.

I take another swig, letting it sit for a moment before swallowing it and pushing my glass forward on the hard rock maple. "It's damn good."

Griffin smiles as he pushes his hair out of his face. I swear when we were younger his dark brown eyes matched his dark hair perfectly. I guess the sun is making his hair lighter down South. His foot doesn't stop tapping on the barstool even if he is grinning like a fool. The nervous energy about him is nothing but excitement.

"You know it's good," I tell him and take in the place. We're at the only table in the brewery. All the shiny metal reflects the lighting from above in the old storage center. It's perfect for brewing. Tall, twelve-foot-high ceilings and a single open space. That's all we need. A place to brew. "Now we just need to get it going and start selling."

"See, that's the problem."

He bought this place and I love it. It's only the first step of many for what we have in store, though. Nailing down the recipes for the beer doesn't matter if:

It isn't a damn good beer.

We can't sell it.

"The beer is good, but we still don't have a license for South Carolina." My best friend shrugs with his gaze fixed downward at the empty glass and lets out a long exhale. It's the first time I've seen him look like this since he moved down here.

"I thought everything was moving along right on schedule?" I ask him, feeling my back lengthen as I sit up straighter. "You set up shop, then I come down and we get to work on the brewery and the bar."

"I set up the brewery and we've got everything we need, but we don't have a license to distribute."

My nod is easy and short as I rub the stubble at my jaw mindlessly. "I thought you got it last week?" With a pinched brow I stare at him, waiting for an answer as unease runs through me.

I had the money, he had the knowledge, and together we had the same dream.

"Just a license is all that's standing in the way, right? We're still doing good on budget."

"Yeah, yeah," he answers and leans back. That restless tapping comes back, though. "We're good on the budget. They just aren't reviewing the application and I don't know why."

"I thought you knew people. Don't you have connections?"

"I'm hardly connected," he tells me. "My uncle lives down here but not in this township. But this is where the money is. The tourism and lots of generational wealth are all here. This is where we have to sell it. I just need a way in so we can get this license approved."

"No connections ... At least you have the accent, though," I say, hoping the joke will lighten things up. Everyone down here sounds different from me. A hint of a twang is part of the Southern charm. It reminds me of a girl I hooked up with when I went to visit Griffin once. My nerves prick at the memory. I can't shake the thoughts of her since I've been down here. I haven't thought about Rose in a while, but this past week, she's been coming to mind more and more. I tell myself it's because Griffin and I came up with this plan back then when I met her.

"All right, well," I say and let out a sigh, my thumb now tapping on my jeans in time with Griffin's foot against the bar. I guess the nervous energy is contagious. "Let's get the hell out of here and see if we can't make some headway at the bar?"

"What are we going to do if we can't get the license?" he asks with his voice low, true uncertainty written on his face. "You want to move the bar to my hometown?" He's younger than me, fresh out of college. Broke as all hell and he spent the last eight months doing all this work, spending all my money. I can tell he needs the payoff. He needs something good to go our way.

With my hand on his shoulder, I squeeze once. "We have the brewery and the recipes, so we can always sell somewhere else, it just means more costs and we'd have to sell the bar ... which ..." Which would be fucking devastating, a time suck, and a waste of money. I don't finish the sentence. I'm not going to kick the man when he's down.

"We'll do whatever we have to do. This beer is better than any of the shit in the liquor stores around here and on tap in their bars." I slap my palm down on the table and tell him, "We worked too hard to go home now."

"You didn't do shit," Griffin says and finally cracks a smile as I slip on my jacket, ready to get the hell out of the brewery that ate up my savings and might have been useless to build down here. That sense of unease from earlier starts to eat away at me again and that tells me one thing: I need to get moving and focus on something else.

"You're going to stay down here, right?" Griffin asks as he stands up, the legs of his stool scratching against the concrete floor.

"Yeah, I think so," I say half-heartedly. My lease ran out when Gramps died and I have no desire to go back home. There's no reason to at all, besides my mom's cooking on Sunday family dinners. She gets why I had to leave, though. She understands how close I was to the old man.

I answer him absently about whether or not I'm staying. "I'll be here at least until we get the liquor license and make sure things are back on track."

Griffin scoffs as he takes the two glasses to a larger basin sink. "That could be a few weeks, or it could be a few months. They approve very few applications for those who aren't from around here and given the lack of response I'm getting ..." he trails off and shakes his head, looking past me at all the brand-new equipment.

"We have the state license. We can sell. Just not in a bar. We'll make it work for now."

Standing straight up, Griffin's my height. It was a running joke among our friend group back in high school that that's why we saw eye to eye. We grew up the same in more ways than that. He's leaner, though, and smarter than me in a lot of ways. I'm good with my hands and I'm willing to take risks that most people don't. Together, we're going to figure this shit out.

"Stop worrying. Some things take time and we've got

that. I'll stay as long as it takes."

"If we don't get that license," he starts to say, continuing to dwell on it as I walk past him toward the large steel double doors, not bothering to stress about something I don't have control over yet.

"Let's head over to the property anyway and see how the construction team is doing." Turning to look back at him I add, "I need a break from beer tasting."

Griffin grins slyly. "Never thought I'd hear you say that."

We shut the doors of my pickup truck without locking them and walk toward our soon-to-be bar. Just seeing it standing there, all wood and stone, but knowing what it will be ... shit, it makes all this stress worth it.

In downtown Beaufort, mom-and-pop stores dot the streets along with white-posted porches of antebellum mansions. A fresh spring breeze tinged with sea salt gently passes us as we pause to take in the location.

The site is an old hardware store we bought with the intent to tear down and rebuild. Our property features a rare corner parking lot in the middle of the downtown area, where space is at a premium, so it was worth every penny. We were able to buy the brewery space and equipment, plus the building lot and construction costs. Up next is the décor and menu, and I sure as hell have a vision for that, plus an idea of the cash needed. But now the license is stalled for the lot to be a legal bar for alcohol, in other words, using the brewery we bought to make an actual income rather than small-scale distribution. With nearly all my savings in these two investments, I need that license yesterday.

Griffin told me going into this that it was a high-risk venture and my answer back was that those are the investments that are high reward. I'm starting to second-guess my mindset going into this. I may have been blinded but I know one simple thing for certain: it's always been my dream to open up a bar near the ocean.

"Good location," I say, keeping it positive as another gust of sea breeze goes by us. Griffin nods, turning to look around as if he's seeing it for the first time when I know he's been down here nearly every day for months.

Shoving my hands into my jean pockets, and listening to the slow traffic running down the street, I pay close attention to this old street that used to be Main Street according to the details on the listing.

Our bar, assuming all goes well, is right next door to an art gallery. Next to that is an event space used mostly for weddings, along with school and corporate events. At the other end of the block is a funeral home.

Whether due to tragedy or celebration, people always need a spot to drink and this is the perfect location for a bar.

The sound of a circular saw reverberates through the place as Griffin and I enter the wide wooden door with iron details. That door was the first thing I bought for this place. Before we even had an address or knew we'd be in this town. That door is what I want everyone to see. It's smoked and worn down. A showpiece of what I want to feel like a modern Irish pub. We've got a simple design for the bar laid out, but we've still got to put those finishing touches on everything that will make it the vision I've had in my head for years.

Griffin and I talk with the contractor and a couple of carpenters about next week's work.

Since he's local, sun-kissed and has that southern twang with a constant charming smile, Griffin blends right in. I, on the other hand, look and sound like a Yankee, or so I've been told. I can't count the number of times I've been asked, "What brought you down here?" in the week I've been here.

As Griffin and I review the plans on the only installed booth with the smell of fresh paint and sawdust all around us, he stops in the middle of his sentence.

"You okay?"

I meet his gaze. "I'm fine. Just imagining this bar filled, with a TV right there," I say and gesture to the far corner. "A college game on and this whole town in here, drinking our beer while they cheer on the home team."

Griffin comically mimics a roar of cheers and a huff of a laugh leaves me.

"Everything's coming together," I say then raise an imaginary glass and click my tongue when he pretends to clink his imaginary glass against mine.

"Missed you, bro," he tells me with a grin.

Nodding, I tell him that I'm glad I'm here with him. Glad isn't the right word, though. I can't shake this feeling that's come over me since I got here. I don't think I like it. But part of me is excited as all hell by it.

It's just nerves. That's all this is. I'm sure of it.

We head outside with the intention of checking out our competition in town, a.k.a. having a few beers around town, and lean on my truck for a few moments, taking advantage of the fresh air and catching some late afternoon rays of sun.

The sound of keys jingling approaches up the sidewalk, and next thing I know a gorgeous woman, petite with long blond hair, walks by us, then waits on the corner for the light to change so she can cross the street.

Griffin is saying something but his voice turns into background noise, my eyes drawn to her like she said my name even though I know she didn't.

The hair on the back of my neck stands up, and an eerie feeling of déjà vu comes over me.

Long strands of blond hair cascade down her back. She wears a pastel floral skirt along with a simple cream tank top to match. I don't recognize her as anyone I've run into since I've been in this town, but I feel like I know her.

The light changes and as I watch her cross the street, something stirs from within me. Despite the fact that I didn't get the closest look, the prick of familiarity with her is so strong.

"You ever see that girl before?" I blurt out, interrupting Griffin as I tip my chin in her direction. It's a small town. He told me once that everyone knows everyone.

He turns his head to get a good look at her and his brow furrows. "Yeah, sure. She's a few years younger than me, I think. My uncle knew her family, or at least he knew her father. Pretty sure everyone did. Magnolia Williamson."

"Magnolia," I say, repeating her name so I can ease my voice over the softly spoken syllables. I don't remember ever meeting a Magnolia. She disappears out of my line of sight and I turn my attention back to Griffin. "I don't know anyone named Magnolia, but she seems familiar."

"Her father ran some faulty investment scheme that went downhill. He lost a lot of money for a lot of people. Then the asshole went and died a few years ago and left her to pick up the pieces. Gum?"

Griffin holds out a stick of Wrigley's gum for me to take.

"No thanks," I say and wave him off.

He squints and looks at me as he shoves the piece into his mouth. "Why so curious?"

I shrug and swing around to the door of my pickup.

"She reminds me of a girl I once knew. But her name was Rose."

CHAPTER 5

MAGNOLIA

P lacing another sold sign on the original piece from a local artist, I let the sense of pride I'm feeling prance into a smile on my face. The new website is working like a dream.

And that was my idea.

A giddy little dance, one that lasts all of five seconds and ends with me looking over my shoulder to make sure no one passing by the empty art gallery was watching, is my reward. That and a bigger paycheck.

The art in the gallery is stunning and photography can't capture it. Video sure does a hell of a good job, though. My black heels go clickety-click on the old worn barn floors of the gallery as I make my way back to the counter. It's the only piece of furniture in this place, bar the two simple white benches at the very front by the twin bay windows. We have art displayed both on the wall and on easels. No drinks are allowed in here so we don't have a reason for tables, unless we're holding an event.

The twelve-foot-high ceilings are white, as are the walls. It's stark and bare, which it should be if you ask me. The art is the point. The art should be everything. Those pieces are the only thing anyone should be looking at in here.

Every square inch of this place is perfect ... because the art is unique, exceptional and fully on display.

It sells substantially better online, though. Especially now that we have videos of each individual piece and a strong social media presence.

Nowadays, everything sells better online according to Mandy. My boss has a generation of experience more than me, complete with darn good taste. She also has a closet and a half of high-end clothes for all her trips up to New York that make me envious of her. And a husband who loves her and two perfect children who are my age but still in college. Graduate school for one, med school for the other.

She's the epitome of what every one of my classmates wanted to be when I was at UD for art history.

Her own gallery, trips to every opening around the world worth mentioning in Aesthetica Magazine ... and the well-rounded social life of a wife and mother. I'm nowhere near her level. I get her coffee, I crunch the numbers and manage the advertising, and in return, she lets me pick the art.

My gaze wanders to the paper cup of coffee I got for her, knowing she'll be in for the weekly meeting in T-minus five minutes.

Mandy offered to pay my way to a handful of out-of-state galas this past year, but I always said no. Bridget is just a little young for me to feel comfortable leaving her for that long. Mandy knows, but she still always asks.

It's e-ver-y-thing when she comes back with pictures and stories about the events and artists. I may be working under her, but I still get to live the dream vicariously through her. One day, I'll be in her shoes. I know I will. Years ago, I may have thought it would never happen, but I've clawed my way past that depression and now I know I won't stop until I'm on top like she is. Until then, she'll get me the new artists I'm dying to feature, and I get to learn everything there is to know about running one of the foremost galleries in the country.

Gulping down at least a third of my far too sugary latte, I smile as I tally up this quarter's sales. She recruited me to get the new website online and trusted me to provide the videos detailing the art along with writing the copy for the website. And I freaking crushed it.

Another five-second happy dance ensues, but this time someone walks by the front, their shadow preventing the afternoon sun from making its way back to me in the middle of the gallery. I plaster a sweet smile on my face, tapping at the keys and doing my best to look professional until the shadow passes.

The silence and the wait remind me of when I first applied for this job. I was terrified to hand in my résumé anywhere in this town, let alone this place, my first choice for a job instead of settling for doing anything else here. It was a dream come true to have Mandy Fields move her art gallery to Beaufort. I didn't have my degree, only three years of higher education under my belt. That wasn't why I was afraid, though.

My father ripped people off for a living. Every member of a board of directors, every family with any kind of financial influence, all lost money by investing with a crook. Said criminal being one Albert Williamson. My father, more than likely, stole from Mandy and her husband too.

It was just as devastating as it was embarrassing. Even worse, it was damning in this small town.

Everyone knew exactly who I was and my situation when I came home early from college to pick up the pieces of what was left. They all knew I'd never had a job and that I was his daughter. Who the hell was I to ask anyone to hire me? Let alone for my dream job.

My worst fear was that they thought I didn't fall far from the tree. Why would anyone employ the daughter of a liar and a thief?

The news broke about my father, and he died the next

day. Two weeks later, I learned there was no money. There was a single bank account with a few thousand in it but the cheat disguised as a bimbo that my father had been sleeping with ran off with it all.

So I had nothing but a tainted last name and bills to pay. I had no experience, and no lifelines left. Mandy wasn't my first option simply because of the shame. Renee convinced me to go for the one job I really wanted in this town. She said all the whispers and dirty looks were mistakes and the people around here would remember who I was and what I was made of. Fake it till you make it and all that. It's her motto and she pushed me to do it. I'm so grateful she did. Robert gave me a place to stay so I could sell my family home and work on paying off debt after debt.

Four years later, this is the only job I've ever had, and with the new website and increased sales, it's paying pretty darn well to boot.

I suck down the rest of my coffee before clicking on an email about the exhibition coming up. We're hosting the event and I needed lodging information from Chandler. He runs the inn a few blocks down.

The rates and blocked-out dates were the last pieces of information I needed to send out a mass email to all invited guests. By the time I'm done thanking Chandler and whipping up a draft of the email, which I forwarded Mandy to check before I send, a new email comes through. It's from Mandy.

She can't make it in today. Darn, I really wanted to brag about—I mean, celebrate the sales. On the other hand, literally the other hand, is her coffee, which I shall gladly drink.

I finish mine and scoot hers closer to my laptop. It doesn't escape me that it's a bit vexing to not allow any drinks in the gallery, even though I drink coffee right here every day.

But I'm a single mother of a three-year-old. I need the coffee if I'm expected to function and unlike patrons, I can't exactly leave just to get a drink when I'm supposed to be working.

Just as I'm replying to Mandy, updating her on several things she should know ASAP, including the details about the exhibit, the door chimes a subtle ring and I hear a familiar voice.

"Why is it always dead in here?" Renee asks in a comical tone that makes me smile. She wanders over to one of the new pieces we just got in from New York. It's abstract circles painted with watercolors on a four-by-seven canvas. The edges have a hint of silver and, in the right light, they look like the phases of the moon.

"She's brilliant, isn't she?" I ask Renee in return, ignoring the question about it being dead in here.

After squinting at the name on the info card next to the canvas, she tells me, "Yeah, Samantha has serious talent." She whispers when I make my way to her, sans coffee, "This would look even more brilliant in my bedroom."

The laugh is genuine, leaving me with a grin. "You wish," I say. With my arms crossed, I admire the painting again.

"I'm doing the video for it today, want to sit in?"

Renee walks to the bench at the front, leaning against it she makes a face that forces my grin to grow wider. "I'd really rather not."

Renee isn't exactly into art. I don't hold it against her because most people like to look at it, but are bored by the details. I get it; I know it's my nerd side. She doesn't hold that against me, which is why we work so well together.

"I was on my lunch break and thought you may be lonely in here. Since, you know, there's never anyone in here."

"I told you," I say, repeating what I've told her a million times, "the sales are mostly online, but we need the space for displaying the art and hosting events."

"So you say," she says and slips out her phone. "I've got forty minutes, want to go to Charlie's?"

I take a peek at my own phone, checking the time and then snatching my newly acquired coffee. Martin won't be here for another two hours. He does the packing and shipping and although I don't physically do anything, he likes to have me around if he has questions about which pieces are which. He's an older man in his seventies and technically retired from the postal service. Boredom led him to apply for the job. I'm glad Mandy hired him; he's got stories that pass the time. So many stories about this small town.

"Charlie's it is," I say. I make sure to lock up, the bells above the door chiming for good measure. As I'm pulling on the handles to double-check it's all secured, Renee asks me about Bridge's first week of preschool.

She's the fun aunt I wish I'd had when I was growing up. It makes me happy Bridget has her. Sharon and Autumn too. The three of them taught me a valuable lesson: friends can be your family.

From the gallery it's only a five-minute walk to Charlie's Bar and Grill. Naturally I brag about Bridge the entire way and it only makes Renee smile.

"That's my girl."

It's a little past noon on a Thursday, so Charlie's is bustling with people. The side patio is only half-full, though, maybe because the spring weather is bit hotter today than it should be.

Gesturing to the square iron table complete with a blue and white umbrella, I ask Renee, "Want to sit here?"

Nodding, she sits before I do. The matching iron chair doesn't look comfortable, but I've been here for hours some nights and I know looks can be deceiving.

"I don't know how you do it all alone." Her downtrodden tone is unlike her and I don't care for it.

I shrug, smiling as I see the side door crack open and Mary Sue steps out, propping the door open with her foot as she digs around in her apron tied at her waist, searching for something. Probably a pen.

"I'm not alone," I tell her and give her a gentle nudge. There were plenty of moments over the past four years where I felt alone, although I'd never tell her that. I think everyone has those moments, though, no matter how many people are around you. Every mother definitely has those moments. It's just a part of raising a child. I don't want pity. Not when it comes to Bridget. She's the best part of my life, my world. I don't need pity because of that. Save it for my bills and family history.

Renee is a freaking mind reader, so I avoid her gaze the moment those thoughts hit me. I stare across the street, noting all the windows that are open at the bakery and making a mental promise to myself to walk that way when I go back to work. I love the smell of freshly baked bread.

Mary Sue Rodding, a sweet redhead with a fresh face and bright green eyes, takes our order. She's waited on me the last three times and she remembered right away that I wanted both a sweet tea and a water, neither one with lemon. Her cousin is the football coach at Fieldview High, where she's on the cheerleading squad.

Her family knows my family. Or knew them, I guess that's more correct to say. I'm the last of the Williamsons and when I get married, poof, that tainted name will be gone. I'll have an extra glass of champagne just to celebrate that victory.

It took me a long time to look anyone in the eye. Mary Sue always gives me a broad smile when she sees me, though.

I think part of it is because she likes me, and part of it is because she likes the big tips I leave her. She's also younger and it's typically the older crowd that has an ... issue with me from time to time.

"So the case is settled, Bridgey is in preschool, you have an exhibition coming up ... anything else new?" Renee asks the second Mary Sue turns to head to the table behind us. I don't recognize the people, must be folks from out of town.

Shrugging, I struggle to think of anything at all. I just feel relieved. For the first time in a long time, everything seems to be going right.

"Ooh, there's something new," Renee says as her face flushes crimson and she winds the tips of her auburn hair around her fingers. She tilts her chin forward and whispers, "Check them out."

I swear her hazel eyes flash when she decides to turn on her charm. My first reaction is to shake my head at her in feigned disapproval. Let's be real, though, I love a good piece of man candy.

I'm half hoping it's someone doing construction on the old hardware store downtown. I know it's in the process of being torn down and I envision a crew of construction workers, bodies glistening in the heat.

My body feels alive with awareness but my heart stutters, somersaulting over itself. I was not expecting to see a man I know.

I recognize his eyes first then his broad shoulders. The flash of a memory lights my body on fire. Thump, thump, my heart comes back to life.

Brody. The hiss of his name moaned years ago ricochets in my memory.

He looks all of the man I remember him to be, with a bit of wrinkles that are new around his eyes. The proof of his age only adds to how handsome he is. He has stubble I can see from here; it darkens his strong jaw.

The smile falls from my face in slow motion. He's looking at me and I'm looking at him.

Oh shit. I suck in a deep breath, clutching the cloth napkin in my lap.

He saw me.

CHAPTER 6

BRODY

There's an undeniable feeling when you meet the gaze of someone who knows you. Take that sensation and multiply it by a thousand, and you still wouldn't come close to what I felt when her blue eyes finally found mine.

I knew it was her. The second I saw her, recognition washed over me. It started at the back of my neck and traveled lower. Taking its time just like she did when she drank me in.

That's exactly what she did. The look in her eyes changed from mournful to longing and then grew hotter, blazing until she knew I saw her too.

Caught in my stare, her lips parted like I'd seen them do before and her eyes went wide. I can practically hear her heart hammering in her chest even though we're across the patio of this restaurant.

"Dude, what the fuck?" Griffin's comment distracts me, pulling my attention from her for just a split second.

His brow is cocked and his mouth open but no words come out. With a gesture of his hand, he silently scolds me for staring her down. It's enough of a distraction, causing enough time to go by for Rose to hightail it out of there, her chair sliding back noisily and nearly falling over. I don't remember a time when I've wanted to kick his ass more than this.

"Mags!" the woman she's with calls out as Rose's floral skirt takes off in a blur.

The iron legs of my chair scrape against the floor as I get up to follow her. It's her. It is absolutely her. Why she's running? I have no idea but every instinct in me forces my muscles to cord and tense so I can follow her while I call out, "Rose?"

"Dude!" Griffin yells out, causing the onlookers who were focused on the object of my own attention to turn their prying eyes toward me. I couldn't give two shits ... if it wasn't for the woman now standing up from her seat and refusing to let me pass. She's blocking my path by the railing, preventing me from running down the steps and around the corner where Rose just took off.

"I don't know who you are," the tall woman says below her breath with her lips barely moving. She's tall and thin but somehow still appears athletic. Her eyes narrow as she looks at me and continues, "But 1 swear to all things holy," the threat very real in her wide wild hazel eyes, "I will scream bloody murder if you go after my friend."

What the hell? This is all like a weird dream.

Adrenaline shoots through my veins. It's ice cold and as shocked as the woman in front of me is. In worn jeans and an oversized hoodie, she's hardly a threat, but she's terrified.

Her hands are up, palms facing me and 1 mirror her body language, glancing behind her to try to find Rose, but she's long gone.

"I'm not going after her," 1 tell her, mimicking the way she said it as 1 catch my reeling breath. Griffin speaks behind me at the same time, startling the hell out of me. "He would never hurt a woman; he's just confused."

We share a glance, but the auburn-haired woman doesn't react. She's still playing defense and I'd bet good money that she'd attempt a tackle if 1 rounded her and made a break in between the table and the railing.

"I'm Brody. 1 just recognized your friend Rose. That's it."

"Well, it looks like she recognized you too," she says, indignation draping a veil over her words until recognition hits her eyes, widening them even more and her breath hitches. She knows who 1 am. 1 fucking know she does. Every ounce of fight leaves her and something else takes its place when she speaks again. "Anyway, looks like she doesn't want to see you ... so maybe you should just sit back down." She doesn't look up at either of us as she reaches for her purse to leave.

"Hey, wait." My voice comes our harder than I wanted it to. None of this makes any sense at all and I'm struggling to finish a single thought.

"What did you say your name was?" Griffin pipes up, acting as my wingman, which gives me time to calm the hell down. All I know right now is one thing and it's unsettling: Rose saw me and she took off. Fuck. What the hell did I do to her? My throat's tight as Rose's defensive line informs us that she's named Renee.

"Renee, I'm Griffin," he says and reaches out his hand as if she'd shake it. Her gaze settles on his hand a moment and I take in the crowd. Every pair of eyes here is on us. Well shit, this is not how I thought this would go down. Not here. And not with the girl I spent hours with years ago, at a time when I needed someone and she seemed to need me too.

This isn't a weird dream. It's a nightmare.

"This behemoth is Brody. He's from up north, that's why he has no manners." Griffin's joke actually makes Renee laugh, although it's short and filled with nervousness. Looking between the two of them, there's something there, but it has nothing to do with me and Rose.

"Her name is Rose, right?" I ask Renee, not wanting to waste any more time. "She lives around here?"

Renee's smile fades.

Griffin elbows me in my side, making me wince and then I

give him a death stare. "You sound like a stalker," he grits out between his teeth, low enough for no one but the three of us to hear. Again, he actually makes Renee smile, although he's looking at me while I'm looking at her and she's staring at him.

Clenching my hands and breathing out slowly, I don't know what the hell to do. So I go with honesty. "A few years ago, I met a girl named Rose and … look, if it's her and I did something to her …" Fuck, what did I do? I've never made a girl take off before. Never in my life has a girl run from me. A deep-seated chill takes over.

"No, no," Renee says and it's genuine, her words spoken quickly to stop my mind from wandering. She seems to catch herself, implying with a shake of her head that I've got it wrong. It's clear she knows the story.

"It's just …" Renee trails off, clearing her throat as a gust of wind goes by and her gaze dances between the two of us. Her cheeks are redder now and her defenses are falling. "Look, if she wanted to talk to you—"

"Hey, sorry, had to get my wallet," a small voice cuts in from behind Renee. The beautiful woman I remember so well doesn't look me in the eyes. Her heels click as she takes her place beside Renee, whose slight relief has vanished.

"My name is Magnolia, not Rose. Sorry," she says, practically choking on her apology, "I think you have the wrong girl."

Renee's head tilts ever so slightly, the corners of her lips turning down as Rose's … or Magnolia's … cheeks turn red all the way up to her temple where little wisps of hair have gone wild from the wind. Or maybe from her running.

I don't bother to respond as the air between the four of us thickens. Griffin, the smart-ass that he is, smiles broadly and offers his hand. "Well, nice to meet you, Magnolia. You can run hella fast in those heels," he jokes and Renee's smile is hidden behind a cough as Magnolia stiffly takes his hand. Hers is so small in his. I still can't speak.

"What did I do?" I ask her, making her chest rise and fall faster.

"Maybe give us a minute?" Renee suggests, turning her shoulder to us as she tugs at Magnolia's elbow.

There's a spark between us when she glances up at me. I felt it when she first noticed me a moment ago, and I feel it now. It's scorching hot even as the wind blows by.

Her hair is pushed to the side, falling across her back from her shoulder and spreading goosebumps along her smooth skin. With the gust comes a hint of her scent. Maybe her shampoo, maybe perfume, I don't know but it carries a memory with it. One night.

"I'm sorry," I say and my throat is tight as the words are forced out. Fuck. I feel like a piece of shit, gazing down at a woman I thought I had a connection with, a woman who obviously wants nothing to do with me.

For a second, I have a thought that calms my racing mind. Maybe she's married. Maybe she doesn't want to admit she knows me or remember that night because she doesn't want to think of that night when she's currently committed and happy with someone else.

Please, for the love of God, please be that. Running my hand down the back of my head and then over my neck, I add, "I'm sorry if I ... I'm just, sorry I mistook you for someone else."

I'm ready to turn around. Ready to say goodbye to her and every wild thought I ever had about the girl who stole me away that night years ago, until she reaches out for me.

She did that.

Her hand on mine. It's the first touch we've had in years and it lights a smoldering fire within me that starts to burn hotter and brighter.

But just as a flame singes the flesh, she rips her hand back when I turn to ask what she wants.

"I ... I have to go, I'm sorry." That's when I see her hand, her ring finger without a single piece of jewelry on it.

"You just got here."

Both Griffin and Renee are silent.

"I just have to go right now."

"Maybe ..." she pauses and licks her lower lip, still not admitting that she is who she is. "Maybe I can see you soon."

With Renee in tow, the two leave, and I watch as Rose, or Magnolia, whatever her name is, glances behind her.

Griffin asks the words that resonate in my own mind, "What the hell is going on?"

Chapter 7

Magnolia

Just breathe through the little whistle. I give myself the command again and the silent relief of air doesn't do a darn thing.

"You have to breathe in through your nose and then exhale through your mouth," Renee tells me, lost in her phone and not even bothering to look up as she speaks.

She's the one who gave me this necklace, a rose gold simple chain with a pretty and chic silent whistle on the end of it that matches the color of the chain. It's quite stylish, but it's supposed to be calming me down.

In through my nose, out through my mouth as I stare at the computer screen for the third time, attempting to pay attention so I can put a sticker on the right piece for Martin.

I'm a wreck. Crying is useless and I don't want to, but my goodness, my heart won't stop racing. I just needed time to collect myself, that's exactly what I thought I was doing. Back on the restaurant porch, on the walk back here and in the hour that has passed since then.

That's what I do, I take time and I process everything. And now that I've done that, I have collected a mess. I am in a horrible mess and I have no idea what to do other than to pray that this is a dream, nightmare, or both. Or that he will suddenly vanish and I won't have to face Brody anymore for as long as I live.

Which ... breaks my heart just a little. Maybe a bit more than a little. Maybe it hurts a lot to even think that years ago when I searched for him and prayed for him to come save me, he was nowhere to be found, and now he shows up?

I used to dream about him and the way he was with me, so sweet and charming, just so I could sleep at night. Because somewhere in the world was someone else who might think differently about me and about my little Bridgey. It was long ago, though; it feels like a lifetime ago. How awful is it now that he's here and all I want is for him to go away?

He looks the same, handsome and charming with a roughness about him ... the images of him at the bar, of us years ago, come to mind. Of the bed he took me in ... My memory did not at all do that man justice.

Sucking air in through the whistle and blowing it back out again, my shoulders rise and fall chaotically. I will not cry, but I don't know what else to do.

"It's for your parasympathetic nervous system, you have to breathe through your nose." Renee keeps her place in the corner of the art gallery, eyeing me pointedly as she readjusts on the floor so she's now cross-legged with her back leaning against the wall. She shouldn't be here and I should focus on working. But Brody shouldn't be here either! That's all I keep thinking. What the hell is he doing here?

Ripping the whistle out of my mouth and making my way to her, past the easels and paintings, I finally come close to the edge of losing it. "You know what I'm not parasympathetic to?"

With the ring of the bell on the door to the gallery, my mouth slams shut, my hands fold politely in front of me and I welcome Miss Jones to the gallery. My smile is fake as can be and I hope she can't tell. I pray she doesn't know anything is wrong, but I would be a fool not to think the entire town will talk and by tomorrow rumors will have spread like wildfire.

It's so very wrong of me, but I'm hoping they're talking about Renee and Brody's friend. Not Brody and me. Please, please, I don't want to be the topic of whispered conversations anymore.

"Miss Jones, can I help you with finding anything in particular, or would you like to peruse? We have a few new pieces over in the more contemporary section," I say and gesture behind me, remembering the last paintings she bought. They were mostly for her foyer, but I think one was for her bedroom.

Miss Jones is quite the spender, not just in here but anywhere she'd like. That's what happens when you've been married three times to wealthy men who either died or cheated, each time leaving her with a heap of cash. Miss Jones is loaded. Hosting parties and wining and dining is what she lives for, or that's what she'd say. Southern hospitality raised her, and she won't let it die.

Tapping a perfectly polished, French manicured nail against her chin, she smiles broadly, the wrinkles around her eyes making her appear ever approachable as she says, "I'm here for a look, dear."

I'd love it if the conversation ended here, not because I don't enjoy waiting on Miss Jones. She's honestly lovely and when I was pregnant with Bridget, she offered to host a baby shower for me. I didn't take her up on it, but it was sweet. She is more than well-off and somehow still manages to be kind.

However, I'd love it if she took her white-jeaned and blue-bloused self out of this store right now so I can have a moment to decompress with Renee.

I've barely spoken to Renee, other than to put her on the task of how the heck Brody got here and how long he'll be here. Thus why her attention has been on her phone and my attention presumably on calming down.

This silent whistle, though, is useless. I hope she didn't

spend a pretty penny on it. It's only worth a dull one found between sofa cushions.

"Nice to see you, Miss Renee, how is your mother?" Miss Jones asks, making conversation as she rounds the counter toward the section of new arrivals.

Her thin lips, painted a shade of pink that's nearly the same as her skin tone, purse as she gets to the first watercolor scenery.

Their conversation is littered with small talk and polite laughter, which I mimic. Making sure to laugh at just the right time, even though inside I feel like my chest is cracking wide open. It's obvious she's prying, but Renee also has a soft spot for the woman. It's easy for Renee to ignore most of the gossiping hens, as she calls them, although she usually adds in other colorful language. Miss Jones gets away with it, though.

My mind drifts as the conversation turns to white noise. Everything was finally okay. I was okay. Bridget is doing so, so well and I felt free for the first time in years.

Tears threaten to prick at my eyes so I resort to turning my back to the two of them and focusing on the computer screen at the desk. As if something is so very important that it's all right for me to ignore a client.

If my boss were here, she'd be livid.

He cannot be here. Brody ... my throat tightens as I take out a bottle of water from under the desk and quietly have a sip.

"Dear, Magnolia, my dear, is the change of weather

getting to you?" Miss Jones asks although I know for certain she knows it's not allergies. "The change of season always bothers me," she continues without pausing and opens the clasp of her purse to produce a small pillbox. "Allergies can be brutal, here you are."

Renee's gaze dances between the two of us as I accept the pill and take it. Why the heck wouldn't I? Better to play along and for Miss Jones to not have any new information to spread gossip. I'm pretty sure the little pink pill was a Benadryl. Maybe I'll get lucky and it'll help me sleep tonight.

"I saw Robert just yesterday," Miss Jones says casually, slipping the pillbox back into her purse as I nearly choke on the sip of water.

Here it is. Here it comes. First she started with Renee and now it's my turn.

"He said his mother's allergies are getting worse. Every season it seems to be something new."

I offer her a smile and answer, "Maybe I've developed an allergy to something."

Renee's grin is Cheshire catlike as she peeks up at me from behind Miss Jones's back. "Roses," she mouths and I swear if I didn't love her, I'd hate her right now.

"Mm-hmm," Miss Jones murmurs, gracefully taking in another piece of art as she continues, "I believe Robert may carry a soft spot for you still." Her voice is quiet, contemplative but still casual. "The way he's helped you, a man doesn't help like that unless he wants more."

Every ounce of blood drains from my face. Oh my Lord, I can't even think about Robert at a time like this.

"I didn't mean to upset you, dear," she's quick to add and the look on her face seems practiced but genuine. The look is one that screams, "I'm sorry I said something alarming, upsetting ... something that crossed the line, but also it needed to be said." I know it well. "I thought we've had this conversation before? No?"

"We have," I say and force a smile although I can feel it waver. Renee takes the moment to stand now, no longer seated and very much paying attention to every word. Bless her, but she doesn't need to be my protector. Well, not from Miss Jones anyway, of all the people in this small town. "I assure you we're only friends."

"Oh, well then," she says with a nod and moves on to the next piece, letting a little gasp show her approval of it, "then maybe that gentleman you happened to run into earlier? Is he a friend?"

"Word gets around fast," I joke, feeling my cheeks heat.

"So he's a friend then?" she asks, glancing behind her shoulder at me before telling me, "I'll take this one." As if this conversation isn't exactly what she came for.

"A friend from your college days, I suspect?" she says and tilts her head, a blush coloring her own cheeks as well. I don't have a moment to answer, not a single moment because just then the bell above the front door chimes and in walks the man of conversation, grabbing the attention of all three of us.

Involuntarily, I reach for the useless silent whistle as if it'll save my life.

There's a saying I never understood: he's a tall drink of water.

The older women around here say it in the beauty salons and at luncheons all the time and it's followed with slight blushing and laughter. I understood what it meant when I heard it; I'm not dense.

The men they were talking about were handsome. Got it, check, understood.

But I didn't really get it until just now. As Brody stands there, slipping his hands into his jean pockets and biting down on his bottom lip like he's unsure of his good-looking self, it hits me.

My mouth is dry and I can't swallow. I can barely breathe, so there's not much in my body that's working at all. Other than the thermostat. One look at him and his broad shoulders, and his strong, stubbled jaw, with the snap of a finger, my insides are all burning up.

It takes a long second for me to close my mouth and gather up the energy to give a polite smile and say, "Welcome." Even the singular word shakes as it drifts into the air.

From the corner of my eye I see two things happen at once.

Miss Jones takes a half step to the right, pretending she's admiring a piece of art I know she hates. "I may take this one as well," she says under her breath. "I'll just have to look at it a minute."

The second thing is that my good friend Renee, really my dearest and closest friend Renee, rolls her eyes. And not at Miss Jones. No, she rolled them at me.

My eyes close as I scold myself. Welcome? Really?

My smile falters but I widen the thing anyway. "Is there anything I can help you with?" My voice is a faux cheery tone and it's obvious even to my own ears. Still, I'm doing the best I can, given the fact that I'm parched and hot and in desperate need of ... that tall drink of water standing there, looking back at me like he may be lost.

"Magnolia." He says my name and it feels like an ice bath drenches me from head to toe. So much so that my toes go numb.

"That's me," I say with my throat still tight, feeling like I'm swallowing down sawdust and pretending I'm just fine. I'm all right. The man who could be the father of my daughter isn't standing right here. I didn't lie to him back then. I didn't run from him just hours ago.

Slipping my fingers around the whistle, I absently toy with it. It would be far too obvious to slip it between my lips and blow right now, but darn do I want to. He takes his time walking to stand in front of the desk where I am. Like a gentleman, he stays on the other side of it, but quite frankly, it's not far enough away.

Everything in this place disappears. There's no big hunk of wood that separates us. Not at all. It's just him with his piercing gaze, and boyish charm. And me, scared and knowing I'm ruining everything. Everything I worked for is going to be ruined by a lie and a secret and there's nothing I can do but to bear the consequences and I hate it. How do you tell a man you haven't seen in years that he has a baby? A sweet baby girl with his eyes. Well, probably. She could be Robert's. Oh my Lord, may the ground open up and swallow me whole.

Both hands wrap around the whistle, my fingers twining together as I try to get the courage to just spit it out. Get it over with. The only thing that keeps me from speaking is the thought that he'd deny her. My perfect little girl. That and the onlookers, and ... well, maybe there are a lot of reasons. Either way, I can't speak. Not a word slips out from between my lips.

"Hey." Brody lowers his voice and glances at Miss Jones. I don't even think he knows Renee's right behind him. She's practically hidden in the corner. "I get it," he says then shrugs and offers me an asymmetric smile that's so comforting and soothing.

It takes me back to that night at the bar, the nostalgic smell of a sweet cocktail and then him. His warmth. His touch. The way he laughed.

I want to hear him laugh. Just to know if my memory is right.

Given the way he looks right now in front of me, my memory hasn't done him any justice at all.

"You all right?" His question brings me back to the present, the here and now of this man I've dreamed of for so long standing so close to me.

"Yes. Yes. What, umm ... get what?" I manage to ask and this time it comes out even. I haven't got a clue how. I clear my throat and say to clarify, "I'm sorry, but you get what?"

"I get why you freaked out. You're a sweet girl. You're from a small town." He nods with each statement, then leans in closer to whisper, as if Miss Jones doesn't have the hearing of a fruit bat. "You don't want anyone to know about your college days."

Oh my God. How is this conversation happening right now? My body blazes again but this time with sheer embarrassment. I know my cheeks are red and my jaw has dropped, but I can't help a single reaction.

In an effort to look anywhere but at his handsome face, I look to my right, which is a mistake because Renee's grin only adds to my chagrin. She sure is getting a kick out of my humiliation.

One breath in, one breath out.

"It's not that," I say then shake my head and manage to look Brody in the eyes.

"It's not?" The smile he's been wearing falls and I wish I could take it back. I wish a lot of things. Wishing isn't going to make this right, though.

"So ... why'd you take off like that? Because you lied about your name?"

I promise I want to answer him, I want the words to come out and just give him the truth regardless of how much of a surprise it is and how much it's going to change everything. The words, though ... they're stuck at the back of my throat and all I can do is stare back at him with a pained look. I've never felt both so foolish and helpless.

"Wait, wait," he says, raising his voice and Renee's brow climbs so high on her forehead it catches my attention. "I have this idea." Brody runs his hand down his jaw and clears his throat before saying, "Hi. My name's Brody. When you left, I asked the waitress what she knew about you because I couldn't take my eyes off of you. She said you're sweet and you're single."

My chest rises and falls as I watch him pretend like this is the first time we're meeting. Like we're starting fresh. His grandstanding is cute and flirtatious, but his nerves are clearly getting to him judging by the way he rubs the back of his neck before asking me, "I was wondering if you want to go out with me sometime."

"Oh, how sweet," Miss Jones comments as if she's innocent and doesn't have a clue what's going on.

"A date?" I ask in a voice that doesn't sound like my own. It's breathless and filled with disbelief.

"If you'd like, I'd really like to take you out this weekend." His voice is lower and filled with a longing I recognize when he adds, "I want to redo this."

"You should say yes to that sweet man, Magnolia." Miss Jones butts in and at that, I roll my eyes. This woman and her pestering are killing me right now.

"Thank you very much," Brody says and flashes her a charming smile. Sweet but completely ignorant Brody. He turns that charm on me next. "So? Will you go out with me?"

Thud, my heart beats in a way that both feels right and like the next beat will take me to death's door.

"Yes, yes," I say and force a small smile to my lips, "let's go out on a date." Even though a part of me is jumping up and down for joy, I cross my arms and the chill across my shoulders doesn't leave me. I'll go on the date to tell him about Bridget and confess everything. Somewhere quiet, where we can talk.

"How about to eat at Morgan's? Have you been?" I suggest and immediately notice Miss Jones's huff of disapproval. I shouldn't be taking the lead, according to Southern etiquette rules, but you know what? She can stuff that huff where it came from.

"I haven't yet, but if that's where you'd like to go, that's where it'll be."

"You said this weekend?"

"That's right," he answers, rocking on the balls of his feet.

"You're staying long then?"

"I might be moving down here." His answer echoes in my head, over and over like a bad replay and in that time, I somehow agree to him picking me up after work on Friday for the date.

With the time and place set, he leaves with a short wave.

The second he's gone, the whistle is between my lips as I hyperventilate.

"Oh my, oh my." Miss Jones has more color in her cheeks than I've seen since the dinner she threw for New Year's two years back.

"Oh my what?" Renee asks, picking herself up.

"We are in for a treat."

"It's not a treat," I murmur and Miss Jones is quick to click her tongue in disagreement.

"Take it from me, dear, I know a thing or two." She gives me a kind smile even though her eyes reflect sympathy. "This is going to be a wild ride. So smile, dear. When you look back on it, you're going to want to remember you did it with a smile."

CHAPTER 8

BRODY

"Is this for some girl?" My mother's tone is grating as I run a hand down my face.

"We talked about this." My mother, she's ... she's lonely. She's been lonely since my dad left her and even lonelier since my grandfather died a few years back. "I told you I wanted to come down here with Griffin and start this business."

"And I told you it was time to settle down."

If it wasn't my mother on the other end of the phone, I'd simply hang up. I'm not in the habit of taking orders from people. I don't like for my intent to be ignored either. My mother's good at both of those. She knows best and all that. But really, she's lonely and she doesn't want me to move away. I hear it in her voice, with her faint upper East Coast accent. She's from New York and never lost the cadence of her hometown.

"You can always come down here," I say to get right to the point, nodding at a template Griffin's holding up. There were five mock-ups a graphic designer pitched for our logo. "That one," I mouth to him, with my mother still on the phone going on about how she can't leave and neither can I. Or at least that's what I hear through it all.

"Mom, you know I love you. I'm still deciding if I'm going to move down here, though."

"And it's not about a girl?" Magnolia's pouty lips and wide gaze flash across my eyes, but I shake it off. I haven't heard from her since yesterday and as far as I'm concerned, we're starting fresh. She's just a girl I'd like to take out and get to know. She's just a girl. Even to my own ears, the statement sounds false.

Breathing in deeply, I joke, "You want me to get married so soon?"

"You aren't a spring chicken, Brody."

Ignoring my mother's comment, I focus on the topic at hand. "I mean it when I say you'd like it down here. You know how Gramps liked to go sailing ... It reminded me of him when I came to see Griffin."

And he believed in me. I wish he were alive to see it all coming together. He'd be proud. Although he'd be on my ass about that license.

My mother's silence strikes a chord in me.

"Just promise you'll come to visit before you decide to be up in arms about me moving down here. I'll even unpack and stop living out of my luggage bags for you." The humorous huff is as good as I'm going to get. I know it.

The sound of Griffin opening up a window in the far right corner comes with an immediate gust of saltwater air. I fucking love it. I take deep breaths in and out as my mother lists all the reasons she can't come down to visit me and how I need to really think about what I'm doing.

It's a damn good thing she can't come down right now, I think, as she keeps talking and I take in the state of this apartment. I figured a three-month lease would work and then once we're settled, if things go well, I might look for something more permanent. It's a simple beige space with no furniture other than the foldout chairs and table Griffin brought down from his parents' basement.

My mother would be livid. Of the list of shit I have to do, though, furniture shopping is low on it. I have a bed in the bedroom at least. A bed and a hot shower are all I need right now.

It takes another ten minutes before my mother sighs and tells me she loves me. Which I knew she would. I'm ever the disappointment to her because I won't settle down.

The second the phone is lowered, Griffin finishes tapping

on his phone, probably writing an email to the graphic designer.

"So I asked Sam, the guy with the sailing boat, and he said we could take it out this Sunday."

Griffin's a damn good friend. Whenever I get off these phone calls, he's right there with a distraction I need.

"I'm down." It's easy to say yes to that. It's one thing I had with my grandfather. Sailing feels like home and Beaufort is one of the coastal sea islands. There's a ton of sport fishing out here. My grandpa would have loved it.

"He said we can bring dates or whomever if we want. Just to make sure to clean up after." Griffin's tone is leading and the beautiful face I pictured only minutes ago at the thought of settling down flashes again in front of me.

Giving him an asymmetric smile, I answer, "I don't know yet. Let me get through the date this Friday first? Or did you want me to ask my girl if her friend wanted to come along and hang out with you?"

"Your girl now?" he asks with a raised brow.

I shrug and say, "You know what I mean." Leaning back in the flimsy chair, I pick up the pile of papers Griffin tossed aside, making sure the option I picked is really the one. I'm relying on a gut feeling, an instinct to go with it. I've followed that instinct all my life and it hasn't screwed me over yet.

"I mean ... if all is well, I'm just thinking it might be a nice second date, is all. And yeah, I think you should invite her friend too."

"If it goes well and she's interested, yeah, I'll ask her," I tell Griffin as he scratches the back of his neck. With his black plastic-framed glasses and slight build, he's always had a little bit of the nerd side to him. He's a good guy, though, and good looking just the same. He should have the confidence to ask Renee to go out with him. Maybe it's just weird for him since I'm seeing her friend. That's uncharted territory for us.

Slapping the final design, the one I'm dead set on, upon the top of the pile, I hand it back to Griffin, who's already nodding. "Yeah. This is the one."

"Damn right it is," I say and get up to grab a Coke from the fridge. "You want one?" I ask Griffin.

"Nah," he says and shakes his head, but he looks uneasy.

"You ready to go?" I ask, shutting the fridge door before I can grab a can. With the blinds rolled up, the sun's given this place enough illumination that I hadn't flipped a light switch on yet today, but now that evening is coming, I turn on the single light in the kitchen and living room.

"I have something else to tell you ... Sam had a little intel on your girl."

"I told you I don't want to know. I'm not looking into her or asking anything other than if she's single." I meant it when I told her we were starting fresh.

"You might want to know this." His fingers tap anxiously on the edge of the computer, folded shut in his lap.

"Go ahead, spit it out," I say casually, grabbing the beverage so my back is to him when he says, "She's got a daughter."

I pause in the middle of opening the can, letting the news sink in and then ask the necessary question, "But she's single?"

"Yes."

"And the dad? Is he in the picture or still have feelings or something?"

"Nope," he says and shakes his head, "she's a single parent."

I never thought I'd feel an easiness come over me at that statement. The can fizzes in my hand and I take a drink, really thinking about it. A miniature Magnolia. She's probably a cute kid. That's when it hits me.

"I bet that's why she freaked. She's a mom now, she can't be running around and having flings."

Damn. I rub the back of my neck but a smile creeps on my face. "That makes so much sense now. And her friend's all protective because of the kid." I'm practically muttering and thinking out loud at this point, but Griffin still hears me and nods.

"Okay so, date this Friday. Sailing on Sunday." Done and done.

"Yeah and you need to get dressed because we have a meeting in an hour for the permits."

"Who's the meeting with?" I ask.

"Some guy close to your age, so I'm thinking he'll be able to pull some strings to get this bar open. Sam said he's a friend of Magnolia's too."

CHAPTER 9

MAGNOLIA

TWO AND A HALF YEARS AGO...

"There's money on the counter," I tell Robert with tears in my eyes, leaving the front door wide open as I cover my face and turn my back to him. Bridget won't stop crying. Every moment she wails, my heart breaks more and more. She cries almost every night around eight and I don't understand why. There are no teeth coming in, she already had a full bottle, and all her naps have been right on schedule. She cuddles when I hold her but still she doesn't stop.

The baby app tells me it's the witching hour. I just want it to stop. My hands tremble when I reach down for her, picking her up out of the pack and play and shushing her even though the white noise machine is on full blast.

"It's okay, little one," I whisper but my poor baby can't hear it anyway over her cries.

"I don't know what I'm doing wrong," I say and breathe out in frustration with tears streaming down my face. I don't know that Robert's heard me until his hand comes down on my shoulder. It honestly startles me. Maybe because I'm exhausted, maybe because I've been alone in this apartment for three days straight, maybe because I feel like I'm going to pass out after lying next to the pack and play for the last half an hour crying right along with Bridget.

"You all right?" he asks and I burst into a laugh that's not a laugh, right before letting out the ugliest sob imaginable.

"This is not your problem," is all I can tell him. "The rent is on the counter," I point out again. That's what he came for. The settlement money I was counting on receiving from my father's estate is being held up and I don't know how I'm going to pay next month's bills if that last property doesn't sell, or if they have to take that money to pay off more debts my father lied about.

"I'm still your friend, Mags. I'm still here for you," he says and his tone is kind, the same as it has been for the last year. Through the pregnancy, through the first weeks after I became the town pariah. He may have left my heart broken, but I'll be darned if he hasn't tried to help me pick up the pieces.

Part of me is grateful for that; part is still angry. And a big part of me wants him to put the pieces back together and hold on to everything. Oh, Lord, the tears are coming back.

"My world is a mess and I don't know what to do." My inhale is staggered and I have to sit down to try to calm myself, but Bridget's screams get louder so I shoot back up.

"Okay, you're doing good, Mags," he says, but his encouragement doesn't help.

"I'm a bad mom," I say, whispering the painful words aloud and then heave in a breath. "I can't help her and I don't know why she's crying. I have no idea."

"You're a good mom." Robert makes the statement as if it's fact. "The bad moms don't even wonder if they're doing a good job." No one's ever told me that. No one's told me I'm a good mom and I nearly burst into tears again, matching my little girl who's still screaming in my ear.

"She won't stop and I don't know what's wrong." My words come out like a plea. I would give anything if she'd just stop crying.

"Sometimes they cry. I'm pretty sure it's like a baby's checklist," he tries to joke and I would roll my eyes but something magical happens.

Bridget seems to take an interest in Robert when he talks. Her cry is hesitant and he picks up a piece of paper, waving it in front of her face. Mimicking a child's voice, he says, "I heard that wittle babies like a wittle wind in their wittle faces."

I let out a laugh, but more than that, a breath of relief. Bridget's head falls back and she shuts her eyes, letting the breeze blow against her face.

Breathlessly, I beg Robert, "Don't stop."

He laughs and continues to wave the paper just above her little three-month-old noggin. "Never thought I'd hear you say that again," he says with a handsome smile.

I let out a small laugh, continuing to bounce my baby girl and I'm grateful for the quiet. Is it that simple? Just a little wind in her face. Probably not, I think. Tomorrow's another day, but it'll pass. It won't be like this for long.

"It's just a phase," I say, reminding myself of what the doctor said.

"And you're a good mom," Robert adds. With a small smile, I meet his kind gaze. "I mean it, Mags. You're doing such a wonderful job."

I wish we could go back. I wish I could change so much. But more than that, I wish I could have him tell me that every time I feel like I'm failing her. I just want to be a good mom to my Bridget. And I wish Robert would stay, but he doesn't.

PRESENT DAY

"I don't want to influence you." As she speaks, Renee has both of her hands up, doing her best impression of a bank teller during a robbery.

I could huff and puff and roll my eyes but instead I'm deflated, and my energy levels are nowhere close to being where they should be. It's not every day you have to break news to someone like I have to. Hey, it's been a few years since we spent fewer than twenty-four hours together ... By the way, my little girl may be biologically related to you. Surprise!

"Can't I just leave him a note?" I half joke, lifting my gaze to the computer screen which should be showing ticket sales for the gallery exhibit but instead it shows social media sites for Brody Paine. A picture of him seated in a foldout chair on the sand of some beach on the East Coast three years ago stares back at me. His tanned skin and cocky smirk light a fire inside me I've been doing my best to smother. "Dear Brody," I say to begin my best impression of reading a nonexistent letter aloud, even holding up the imaginary piece of paper as if I can see it. "You're a father. I should have told you sooner but I couldn't find you after I bailed college to come home to a scandal that ruined my name and made my life hell. I've only just now found my place in this life, but congratulations, you're a dad. At least I'm pretty sure, since her eyes look just like yours."

Renee stifles a laugh with the cuffs of the sleeves to her favorite navy blue zip-up hoodie that boasts a heart in the upper right corner along with the words, "How about no?" With her leggings and gray tank underneath, I know she's wanting to go on her run. She does that, all the working out and physical things. I, however, have a three-year-old. If I'm running, it's because I'm chasing my little girl who probably stole a Sharpie off my desk.

"If you want to tell him, tell him." Renee shrugs and a more serious tone takes over. "If you want to give him a note, do that."

"What if I don't want to do either?"

"You don't want to tell him at all?" Renee's expression doesn't display confusion or judgment. She doesn't even ask the question as if it's a question. It's just a matter-of-fact statement.

"You can get to know him first. If you want. You don't have to tell him the second you see him. These are … unprecedented occasions."

"You make it sound so easy. Don't tell him, take your time, when you do tell him he won't be resentful or in denial at all." My sarcasm drenches the sentence.

"Resentful?" Renee says and scoffs, tossing her head back and taking a seat against the window to the gallery. It's empty, as per usual. But in twenty minutes a man will be walking through those doors to pick me up and I haven't got a clue how to have this conversation with him.

"He has no right to be resentful."

"He does too. He had a child for years and didn't know," I say, defending the sentiment. I'd have a hard time not feeling a certain kind of way about that if our situations were reversed. "I'd want to know—"

"You tried," Renee says, cutting me off. "Maybe you

forget, but you tried like hell when you were already going through hell."

My fingers wrap around the thin wristwatch that used to be my mother's. I check the mother-of-pearl face of it only to find another whole minute has passed. Minute by minute, I keep checking and I don't stop.

"You did your best, Mags," Renee says, her voice full of emotion when I don't respond.

With a long inhale, I nod. "I did my best." Why does it never feel like it's good enough?

"And you've done a damn good job." Renee nods as if agreeing with herself.

"I'm going to blow this, you know? I'm going to sit down and blurt it out and he's not going to believe me." That's my biggest fear. That Brody won't believe me. Or that he won't want anything to do with Bridget.

"Then that's on him," Renee says and she sounds so sure. She's so very certain of everything.

The only thing I'm certain of is that it's going to hurt. Regardless of what happens, this is going to hurt.

Shaking out my hands and then rubbing my clammy palms on my floral high-waisted skirt, I calm myself down. Until the bell dings and I lift my gaze to see Robert standing there. I look him over from head to toe to find he's in a tailored gray suit without a tie, his crisp white dress shirt unbuttoned at the collar.

He's freshly shaven and when he walks up to the counter,

leaning against the top of it with his forearms, I catch a whiff of his scent. He smells like sea breeze and old memories.

Oh nooooo. He needs to go right now. It's hard enough having to face Brody. Having to face Brody in front of Robert? Nope. He needs to go back right through that door he just came from.

"Busy as usual," he jokes with a grin and then waves at Renee as I force myself to huff a laugh.

"And what brings you to this humble establishment?" I joke back, keeping the smile on my face. It comes naturally, but the turmoil roiling inside of me from head to the bottoms of my tippy-toes begs me to spit out the secret. To cut off whatever it is he has to say and spill my guts and tell him to hightail it out of here. I've told him everything all my life. I've told Robert things I've never even told Renee. Although that truth is the same reversed. Renee knows things no one else does either. The two of them are my rocks and I try to be theirs. It's as simple as that.

"I was supposed to have a meeting with a guy yesterday. I think you know him?" Robert's sharp blue eyes are curious as he says the name I dread to hear, "Brody Paine."

"Uh-huh," I answer him, pulling away from the counter and returning to the computer. "What about him?" I ask as if it's casual. As if there isn't a month's worth of dirty laundry ready to be dumped out over his head just from the mere mention of that particular name. Brody.

"Are you seeing him?" I don't expect Robert's question or for him to be so blunt. Neither does Renee, although she only peers up from her phone and remains silent. This counter is my defense; that phone is hers. But neither will save me from this conflict.

"Seeing him is a phrase for it ... I guess." I swallow the truth down, deep down. My plan of action is simple. Brody is told first. I tell him tonight. Then the world can know and judge.

Right now, as much as I don't like it, Robert is grouped in with the rest of the world. Even if it does make me sick to my stomach. Lies will do that. They eat you up. At least that's what my grandmother used to say. She knew what she was talking about.

"Tonight?" Robert asks, leaning forward to get a good look at my outfit. Rose gold heels to match my earrings, and a loose navy blouse tucked into the watercolor floral skirt.

"You guessed it," I practically answer in a singsong cadence. As if it's not a big deal. I've gone out a few times on a date here and there. It never amounts to anything. It's a polite answer to nice guys who want to take me out. I've never really been interested. My hands are full as it is.

This is different, though, and the tension that lies between Robert and me as he stands there across the desk waiting for me to look back at him is evidence of that.

"How do you know him?" His tone isn't accusatory, but the comments in my head sure as hell are.

Shrugging, I try to hide my harsh swallow. "I think his friend went to school back in Delaware."

"That it, Mags?" he asks me and when I look up at him, there's a hurt and uneasy expression in his eyes, and I start to question if Brody told him something. If Robert knows. I want to be the one to tell him. I can't let him find out from the rumor mill. But just as the dam breaks inside of me, Renee pipes up.

"Why's it matter, Rob?" Renee asks. "Were you planning on asking out your old high school flame?"

A very common sigh of frustration leaves me as she chides him. He knows that she knows about our thing. She knows he knows that she knows. And they do this shit all the time pretending like neither of them knows anything about the occasional fling Robert and I have whenever Robert behaves like anything more than an ex and landlord.

Renee's right, he doesn't have a right to ask any questions about my dating life when he lets the world believe we're only friends. Yet I'm choosing to sleep with him, and deep down I know I need to be honest with him if ever I were to … have a romantic relationship that led past dessert. Same goes for him too.

"I'll let you know if it's anything more than that," I answer Robert sincerely before the two of them can butt heads. "For now, it's just dinner," I tell him and saying those words brings a pang of heartache I don't expect. I made a promise earlier to Renee that I'd at least wait until after appetizers to say anything about Bridget. For one, he'd have to stay to pay the bill, right? So he'd be forced to at least process it for a moment. And for two, I'm going to need to eat something in order to sit upright and speak the truth.

Robert looks like he's going to say something, his lips parted and his brow furrowed above his questioning gaze, but he doesn't have a chance. The bell ringing above the door interrupts him and in steps the topic of conversation himself.

Wearing khakis and a light blue polo that actually matches my skirt quite nicely, I know Brody dressed up. Brown dress shoes and all. He's still got that blue collar feel to him with the top of his hair a bit messy and rough stubble lining his strong jaw. Thump, thump, my heart races in my chest and it's far too hot all over the place. I can't escape the rise in temperature.

Oh my Lord. Please. Please, help me to keep on breathing. Both of these men in this gallery suddenly makes it feel oh so small. It's suffocating.

"Hey Magnolia," Brody greets me with a wide and charming smile. He's so unsuspecting when he glances at Robert, offering him a smile. I can tell he's about to walk over to where we're standing and strike up a conversation.

Oh, heck no. No, no, no. Rushing around the side of the counter, I practically sprint out to meet him and hook my arm around his.

"I'm all set," I say evenly although I don't know how. I've never been graceful. I've never been ... ooh, what's the word ... calm under pressure ... hmm, my grandmother used to call it something but all I can think right now is that I need to get the two of them the hell away from each other as quickly as possible.

"Have fun, lovebirds," Renee calls out and I catch Robert's glare at her comment as I pull a questioning Brody to the door.

Robert doesn't say goodbye and I don't either, but he doesn't let me leave without one more remark. "You look good, Mags." Robert's statement doesn't go unnoticed by Brody, who merely lifts his left brow as my cheeks flame. It's not until the door closes behind us that I can breathe. Even then, it's staggered.

"He's right, Mags," Brody says and then rests his splayed hand at the small of my back for only a second to lean closer to me and whisper in my ear, "You look beautiful."

Oh, my heart. My poor, dumb, ready-to-be-torn-to-shreds heart.

Chapter 10

Brody

There wasn't a single second I was nervous back then. The memories of the bar years ago filter in and out as I wait for Magnolia to come back to the table. I know damn well, I wasn't ever nervous.

Maybe when I thought she was leaving me ... maybe then there was an ounce of it. But as I sit here, staring between the lit candles and the double doors to the restrooms, the silver fork in my hand tapping restlessly against the white tablecloth, I'm nervous as fuck.

When the hell did I become this guy?

Running my hand down the back of my neck, I note that it's hotter in here than it should be, or at least it feels like it is and that's not helping any.

Morgan's smells like melted butter and the perfect steak seasoning. Given the classic décor I saw online, I thought Magnolia was right and this place would make for the perfect first date. The pictures on my phone didn't do it justice, though. Maybe this is too much, too classy.

I don't know. Something just feels off.

Not trusting myself to speak since something seems to be lodged in the back of my throat, when she reenters the room and glances around, searching for where the waiter sat us, I lift a hand in the air, waiting for her doe eyes to meet mine. When they do, it all seems to calm.

Everything is normal again. Everything's fine. Why? Because she smiles, soft and sweet and only takes her gaze away from mine to tuck a strand of hair behind her ear and pretend like she's not blushing.

My pulse slows and it's all right. She's here and whatever the hell came over me simmers down.

"You really do look beautiful tonight," I say and I'm proud that it comes out as smoothly as it sounded in my head. With an asymmetric grin on my face, Magnolia lifts her gaze to mine, taking her seat in the booth across from me. I silently thank whoever's in charge up there for not giving us chairs. I would have pulled it out for her if we were … if I wasn't stuck right where I am, watching her practically glide in. "I'm not just trying to make you blush," I add and she huffs a small laugh, shaking her head and looking away for just a moment.

"Compliments will get you nowhere," she replies with a smile and a playfulness I remember. But then her eyes drop to the water goblet, where her fingers rest on the stem and her simper drops too.

"Listen," Magnolia starts to say, a more serious tone now present in her voice, laced with something that sounds like an ending you don't want to hear.

I'm saved by the waiter, who comes just then to ask her what she'd like to drink. He knows her by name. Everyone around here seems to know everyone by name.

Griffin wasn't wrong about that.

"The Green Tea," she answers and the second the waiter is gone, I don't give her a chance to continue whatever she was going to say before.

"Green tea? You don't want a drink?" My gaze travels from my beer, the beads of condensation growing on the tall glass, and then back to her.

"The Green Tea is a cocktail," she tells me with a smile before taking a sip of water. "With vodka."

"Ah," I say then lean back in my seat and nod. "That's more like it."

There's a moment of quiet. It's comfortable at first, but then just like when she sat down, her smile fades.

"There's something I have to tell you." Her voice cracks at the very end and I can't stand the look in her eyes. Maybe she doesn't notice that her hands fall to her lap and her shoulders hunch inward at whatever she thinks is so damn important. But I notice and I hate it.

"Now hold up," I say, thinking as fast as I can on my feet, all those jitters I was feeling coming back to me. "I have a proposition."

"A proposition?"

With a single nod, the smile is weak on her beautiful face, but it's there, just barely.

I clear my throat when the waiter comes back. I think his name is Nathanial. Tall and lean, with dark scruffy hair but everything thing else on him is clean cut.

"Do you two need another minute?"

"Yes please," Magnolia answers for us and I can only stare at her. Whatever's on her mind feels like an ending. Like the last page of a story that never really had a chance.

I don't accept it.

Before she can say whatever she was going to say with those beautiful lips parted, I make my move.

"Pretend it's all new. Would you tell someone you just met whatever you're about to tell me? Like it's okay for first date conversation?"

"But you aren't someone I just met," she says insistently. Her small hands come back to rest on top of the table as she squares her shoulders, dead set on telling me whatever it is that's on her mind.

"Look," I say, cutting her off before she can speak again. "I want a chance, Magnolia." I don't know why I'm begging her. I question my own sanity. There's just something about her. There always was. And I see how she smiles when she looks at me. That has to mean something. "All I want is an honest chance. I'm a different guy than I was back then and there are things you don't know about me. Just get to know me, give me a shot before you say whatever you're about to say."

"How do you know what I'm going to say is bad?" Magnolia asks me, but she can't even look me in the eye. Instead she lifts the menu on the table and stares at it. The one with the chef's specials for the evening.

"Because it takes your smile away ... Because you look like you're going to tell me no."

With a gentle shake of her head, the loose curls sway slightly as she says, "It's not a no."

"But it's not an honest shot."

She doesn't deny my statement. A moment passes and Nathanial comes back with her drink and then takes out his pen and paper. Before Magnolia can ask for more time, I order. Appetizer included. Which gets a mumble of something from Magnolia, but I don't make out exactly what she says.

She follows my lead, ordering the item on the menu I was kicking around getting, but I decided on the ribeye instead. The second he's gone, Magnolia glances at me, really debating something.

Setting the menu down, Magnolia leans forward, her forearms braced on the table, looking all types of businesswoman as she stares at me.

"All you want is a chance but you don't know what you're getting a chance at," she finally says.

"Then tell me about yourself. Tell me what I've missed. And I'll tell you the same. Just don't shut me out before it's even started. Because the way you look at me, it's like you have something that's going to end this thing. And we haven't even gotten started."

My plea is just that. Griffin would laugh his ass off if he saw how much this woman had me by the balls. Shit, any grown-ass man would. That weekend Griffin called me up to watch his place ... I know he did it because I needed to get away. And there she was, the distraction I needed.

A second passes and then another. She takes a sip of her drink and leans back in her seat.

"I'll be honest. I don't remember much from that night, other than I really felt good next to you. I remember laughing and I remember kissing you and everything after," she reminisces with a softness to her voice, like she longs to go back. "So tell me everything, Brody. You tell me first and then I'll tell you."

"Back and forth. Tit for tat," I say.

"Tit for tat," she agrees, taking another sip.

"I came here because I wanted to sail," I offer up first.

Sailing is something I did with my grandfather. I leave that part out. I know eventually I'll tell her, because he's why I was there all those nights ago at the bar. She doesn't know it, but she saved me that night. I'll tell her, though. I'm saving it for whenever she tells me what she thinks is so damning.

"You sail?" The pep in her voice makes me grin. With a nod I tell her I love it.

"I do too." Her response comes complete with a little wiggle in her seat as she seems to settle back. "I've always lived here. Except for when I was in college, of course." She stirs her drink as she adds, "So I've been sailing more times than I can count."

"Same ... well, not about living here." I guess she likes the way I add in the correction because she laughs and leans in, ready for more. The conversation is easy, the atmosphere gentle and coaxing. Any tension that was present before vanishes. She kept her word, giving me my chance.

"I'm going sailing this weekend. Come with me," I say, inviting her with all the confidence I have and that requires a sip of beer and then another as she hesitates to answer.

"Sail away with you?" She laughs softly into her drink and the waiter comes back just then. Nathanial asks if she'd like another drink.

I know I have her when she nods a yes.

"My buddy Griffin is coming, but it's just us. Soaking up some sun and maybe taking a dip."

"Mm-hmm." Magnolia's attention leaves me as a rectangular plate of bruschetta is placed in front of us.

She's more than eager to take a piece and I join in. The crunch of the toasted bread and drizzle of balsamic is addictive.

"Good, right?" she says and grins around the last bit from her small piece, then pops it in her mouth.

Something about her smile, about the way she licks the tip of her finger afterward has my cock twitching in my jeans. She makes me feel like I'm in high school all over again. Like I'm some puppy dog she already has on a leash.

"Damn good," I respond and let my gaze fall a little south of her chin. Her laugh brings a wide smile to my lips and she pretends like she's going to toss her napkin at me.

This is exactly what I remember from that night. Not the conversation, but the feeling that stirs inside of me.

I wanted her, and she wanted me. That's really all there was to it. With a soft hum and her posture more at ease, I give her a compliment, telling her, "I like your hair that way."

She brightens and with the way her hand twitches, I bet she'd have touched her hair to help her remember how she did it if she wasn't so self-conscious.

"Sun-kissed, I mean. It suits you." The blush on her cheeks is sweet and it makes me smile.

"There's a little more sun down here than up north, huh?" I love that hint of a Southern accent in her voice.

"That's not the only reason I like it down here," I say,

letting my voice drop and wink at her.

"Stop," she says and blushes again, more vibrant and bashful.

"There's also sailing. Don't forget," I add, toying with her still and she outright playfully smacks me. The sense of ease is settling between us and everything is feeling more right than it has before now.

"Just kidding," I tell her and snag another piece of bruschetta.

As she laughs, I'm drawn back to that moment years ago, when she fell into my arms and then into bed with me. So many nights I've dreamed of those soft sounds that slipped from her lips back then.

Before I can get too lost in the memory, she carries on the conversation after taking another bite of the bruschetta.

"How'd you guys meet?"

"Me and Griffin?"

"Yeah."

"Don't think I didn't notice that you didn't answer my question about coming sailing with me. You could bring Renee," I offer to sweeten the deal.

She laughs, but still doesn't answer. Her legs sway slightly and she seems to contemplate it.

"I'm pretty damn good at sailing," I tell her. "Promise I won't crash."

Although that gets me another laugh, she asks another question, rather than answering. "When's the last time you went?"

"It's been a bit."

"How long's a bit?"

"Too long. I've been really busy. Probably two years now. And the last time was the only time that year."

"And you're sure you won't crash?" Yet again she follows up with another question, but judging by her tone, I'm almost certain she's going to say yes.

"Cross my heart, I won't crash."

With a shy smile and not an ounce of that tension she had when she first sat down, she agrees to another date. "All right then. Sailing sounds like it could be fun."

My grin is genuine and inwardly I pump my fist in the air. It's a win. Another chance to show her who I am and find out more about this girl, the enigma that she is.

The rest of the night is just as relaxed. It's almost like two friends who lost touch catching up. Although the small touches and the way she blushes certainly aren't reserved for friendship. There's a desire, a sense of want, and I feel it too. Just like the first time I met her.

The only thing I'd change if I could would be the way she dodged the goodnight kiss. Instead she left me hanging with a feminine chuckle before telling me she'd see me Sunday for sailing, reminding me that I'm not allowed to crash.

CHAPTER 11

MAGNOLIA

"I'm not allowed to have the Green Tea from Morgan's anymore." As I mumble into my phone, I roll over on my bed so I can watch Bridget stack the blocks. She's been up since 5:00 a.m. and won't go back to sleep.

Her curls bounce as she plays and she's quiet and happy. It is what it is. Today I'm a tired mama.

"Oh, don't blame the alcohol."

"It's absolutely the alcohol's fault." My words are a grumble and they fall flat. As flat as an open soda can left out overnight.

"Come on," Renee says, trying to coax me, her chipper positive side coming out against all my doom and gloom. "We talked about this. You weren't going to tell him. We decided that."

"No," I say, correcting her. "I decided I was going to tell him. Whether or not you want to ignore those texts I sent is on you. I was supposed to tell him. Come clean and make sure he knew." It couldn't wait for appetizers. But then again, apparently it could.

There's a featherlight weight constantly fluttering in my chest. It hasn't stopped and it gets in the way of my heart beating right. Worse than that, it hurts. I can't stop staring at my daughter, knowing what she didn't have. But also what Brody didn't have. And I'm keeping it from him.

"First off, it's been one date. Don't be so hard on yourself. A PG date is hardly a time to drop a bombshell." I roll my eyes at her "PG" comment and pick at the comforter. The last thing I wanted to do was lead him on. PG was the best I had to offer him.

"I've seen him three times now. The initial bumblefrick of a meet. At the gallery and then for two hours on a date." There's no excuse. The last statement goes unsaid because it's stuck at the back of my throat as the guilt strangles me.

"You will tell him," Renee insists and I nod at the ceiling in agreement. "You have every intention to ... when the time is right." I find myself nodding along with her.

Stretching my back, I take my time to sit cross-legged on my bed, balancing the phone between my ear and shoulder. The creak of the bed with my shifting weight gets Bridget's attention. "Mommy tired," my three-year-old tells the baby doll she's propped up in front of my nightstand. Lifting the doll she aptly named "Dolly," Bridget shakes the doll slightly as she commands me, "Go bed, Mommy. Is nap time."

A soft chuckle leaves me and all the weight of the date two nights ago seems to dissipate.

As Bridget returns to stacking blocks, Renee lists all the reasons I don't have to tell him anything. Including the fact that he could be a serial killer and that Bridgey doesn't need that in her life. I don't think my eyes could roll any harder. Without giving her a response, I take in what Bridget's building on the floor next to the bed. I think it's a castle.

"You're going to be a little engineer, aren't you?" Renee hears me on the other end of the phone and asks if she's playing with the blocks again. "Mm-hmm."

"The Lego kind or the wooden ones?" I know she's asking because she got her the wooden ones and Robert got her the baby Legos. That constant lightweight feeling in my chest grows heavier at the reminder of Robert and how he fits into all of this. He knew there was a chance the baby was his and that was reason enough to help me back then. Even though I told him I'd been with someone else.

When I was pregnant, I told him there was a chance she wasn't his and that she wasn't his responsibility. My sweet daughter distracts me once again, bless her heart, as she picks up Dolly and knocks over every single block in the tower.

Her shriek of happiness and the smile on her face is complete with what sounds like an evil laugh.

"She's playing with the blocks you got her, and she's not going to be an engineer ... she's going to be Godzilla." Again I find myself smiling, even in all this emotional turmoil with no easy outcome.

"For real, though, I want to tell him ... I should tell Robert too."

"Robert?" The single word comes out like the most offensive curse.

"I don't like secrets," I say and the confession slips out a little lower and sadder than I intend.

"It's not a secret. It's just—"

"It's just what?" I throw myself back on the bed and make sure my tone stays upbeat for Bridget's sake. Her little ears hear everything. "It's a secret. Robert should know and so should Brody."

"It would be different if you were in a serious relationship. Robert uses you—"

"And I use him too," I'm quick to reply, defending him.

Renee pauses for a moment and then repeats herself, the same serious tone taking over. "It would be different if you gave either of them the impression that you were looking for something serious. Robert uses you and Brody may be gone in a week for all you know. You have to protect yourself and your daughter. Tell them when you're ready and the blowback is minimal."

"Blowback?"

"What if Robert throws you out?"

"He wouldn't do that and you know it." It's offensive that she would even say that. Robert is my friend and has always been there for me. I know she wishes things were different, but if I had to get over it, so does she.

"What if Brody's the father and he leaves you and then Robert leaves you too?"

"He said his bar is going to be where the old hardware store was." I remember the conversation last night. We could have talked for hours, but I had to get home for Bridget and also make it clear that I wasn't looking for the same thing I was looking for years ago. "They're just waiting on paperwork."

"And?" Renee pushes, adding, "It's his friend's name on the paperwork. Not Brody's."

"What?"

"You know I have friends in all the right places. For all we know, Brody could be lying about sticking around. He could hightail it out of here the second you mention Bridget."

My throat's too tight and itchy, just like the back of my eyes are with the tears threatening to fall at how blunt Renee is.

"You need to protect yourself and your daughter. So when you feel the time is right and safe to do so, you can tell them and they aren't entitled to a second sooner than that."

"Right." I manage to get out the single word. "But what's

the difference between today and tomorrow? Nothing's going to change. There are always going to be those risks."

"What could change is how much you know Brody."

She's got a point. The little devil on my shoulder nods as I bite down on my thumbnail. I can only nod, gathering up my composure as I watch Bridget stack the blocks once again. She's my everything and we'll be fine with or without them.

Renee's right. It's not serious with the men in my life. But Bridget's upbringing is serious and I need to know more about Brody other than that he makes me laugh. The way he looks at me makes me blush. And I love it when he takes a drink of beer because he licks his lower lip after and I find it to be the sexiest thing I've ever seen.

"Word around town is that you two had a good night."

"He tried to kiss me at the door."

"Your front door?"

"No." My smile widens as I remember the night. "He didn't want to do anything that might tarnish my reputation. So he got me an Uber to take me back home and he tried to kiss me goodnight on the sidewalk outside the restaurant."

"What a gentleman," Renee says and I can hear her eye roll in the comment. He's trying, I think to myself.

"He really thinks I freaked because I'm ashamed we had a one-night stand years ago." I laugh at the ridiculousness.

Silence from Renee and a squeal of delight along with the clatter of falling blocks from Bridget. "He invited me to go sailing with him. Technically he invited both of us. I could tell him then."

"That sounds like a good plan. I'll watch Bridget while you're out, I don't want to get in between that." I almost bring up Griffin, but she continues before I can say another word. "If you feel like it's right, you can tell him you have a daughter. See how he reacts to that."

"That sounds like a white lie, Renee." The scolding is evident in my tone and Bridget glances up at me. I plaster on a wide smile and reach down, letting my sleep shirt ride up so I can snag a stray block and toss it onto her pile.

"I'm going on this date and I'm going to tell him."

"Okay, okay," Renee says, giving up the fight. "Tell him. But wait until you're back on land to tell him. Just in case he really is a serial killer ... a rather handsome and seemingly sweet serial killer who makes cute babies."

CHAPTER 12

BRODY

"I wish your grandfather taught me how to do that," Griffin calls out and his voice is almost lost in the salty breeze as I tie the rope.

He's already one beer deep, lying back on the deck chair and soaking up the sun. Not that I'm not getting sun myself. It's too hot for my shirt so I'm only in my board shorts as I get the rig ready to set sail.

"Yeah right. Like you'd be helping and not doing exactly what you're doing now." My joking response gets a laugh from him. Being out here this early has reminded me of one thing: I love sailing; I love this boat too. If Sam is serious about selling it, I may buy it from him.

My grandfather would have loved it. When he passed four years ago, I thought he might leave me his boat. He did, but he left a lot more than just that.

I had all the money a twenty something could need to start up whatever company I wanted or sail around the world for a year traveling. That didn't do a damn thing to help me get over it, though.

His passing was sudden and unexpected. It's something I may have come to terms with now, but I'll never "get over it."

I kept his handwritten note to me from the will in my pocket for years and barely touched the money. It took me a while to get back on a boat again, but I couldn't bring myself to sail it. It's his and he's the one who should be sailing it. Maybe I'll bring it down here. So many maybes are sounding off in my head recently.

"Any update on the permits?" I ask Griffin as I step down from the deck to meet him for a beer.

"Not yet." His answer is accompanied with the pop of a bottle cap and then it clinks, the thin metal hitting a bucket to the left of Griffin's cooler. Two meetings now have been cancelled and pushed back. We just need the meeting to actually happen. Politics are frustrating the hell out of me.

"All right," I say and it's all I can answer, not knowing how long these things usually take. It's the weekend, and I'm certain there isn't a bureaucrat willing to work on the weekend when they could be out on the water. Although for a new bar and a decent beer you would think they might sign a paper or two. A huff of a laugh leaves me. "We'll get it soon enough."

Taking a sip, I look out to the horizon, trying to ignore the anxiousness of getting the bar up and running. I can already see Magnolia walking through the front doors, her blue eyes widening as she takes in the place.

With an asymmetric smile curling up my lips, I nod again at Griffin when he agrees, "Soon. It'll all go through soon."

My gaze follows the shades of pink that blend seamlessly into the early morning horizon. It's time to set sail, as my grandfather would say. I swear, every time we went out, he'd announce it just before pulling up the anchor. That's one memory of him I'll always have.

"Well, good morning," Griffin calls out behind me, bringing me back to the present. With his beer lifted in salute, I turn to see Magnolia, a slight blush in her cheeks.

The dress she's wearing over a simple white bathing suit that hugs her curves delectably, is nearly sheer. It's only a cover-up with a dark blue paisley design and the color matches both the flip-flops she wears and the rim of the sunglasses propped up on her head, pushing back her beautiful blond locks. Her wavy blond hair sways as she comes close to the boat on the dock.

It takes a subtle kick from Griffin to get me moving to help her board.

"Twenty footer?" Magnolia asks casually, slipping her glasses down and pushing her hair out of her face. A white straw sun hat is in her right hand with a purse in her left, but she's quick to slip that to her elbow so she has a spare hand.

"Twenty-two," I tell her and hold out my hand for her to take. The second her soft hand reaches mine, heat travels through me. Small sparks ignite and judging by how quick she is to board and let go, and how her bottom lip drops before a simper appears on her beautiful expression, she felt it too.

A moment passes with her glancing at my hand, avoiding my gaze, and looking past me at the sunrise. "It's beautiful." I almost miss her comment altogether, the wind picking up and carrying away the words.

"Look at you, Miss Southern Belle." I hadn't noticed Griffin standing in the cockpit. "Welcome aboard," he says, greeting her with the charm I typically have.

Running a hand over my hair, I watch him help Magnolia down to sit across from him before eyeing me with a look that says, "What the hell, man?"

Yeah, I know. She's got me off my game.

I don't know what it is about her. Maybe the chase, maybe the memories of that night and the fact that the chemistry is all still there. I don't know, but whatever it is, I need to shake it off.

Griffin's not exactly the best when it comes to charm, so the fact that he's one-upping me is a sign that things are bound to go wrong.

"Just to be clear, I plan on getting a little sunbathing in." I don't miss how Magnolia's gaze drops to my chest, then my abs, as I prepare the boat. "If that's all right with you," she adds and her voice is lowered, once again her gaze refusing to meet mine.

"Me too," Griffin says, taking his shirt off and grabbing the sunscreen.

With the two of them getting comfortable, I go through the motions and Griffin joins me, doing his part and leaving the sunscreen with Magnolia.

It's only once we're out, the waves lapping at the sides of the boat that Magnolia speaks up. "You weren't kidding," she calls out above the sounds of the ocean that surrounds us.

"What's that?" I yell back against the wind, still manning the steering wheel. We're not heading out far, just a bit of privacy and open air is all we want.

When she stands to make her way to me, she slips off the cover-up, tossing it on top of her clutch and hat that now sit beside the cooler in the cockpit.

"You're pretty darn good," she says and this time there's no sound at all except for the sweet compliment that comes from those lips. She stands closer than she needs to, her arm brushing against mine and with a slight rock of the boat against stubborn waves, she braces herself against me, but quickly rights herself. I'm grateful for the contact, though, and the fact that she wants to be here next to me.

"Well thanks. I'm glad you came to see me in action." I smile and try to think of something to say, something charismatic, but not a damn thing comes to me. She's breathtaking, she's sweet ... but she already knows that. Our gaze is locked and I know she's waiting on something else as the salty air whips by us and she leans closer to me, her fingers brushing against the wooden helm although she doesn't try to take it over. She's just feeling her way.

"Does everyone call you Mags?" Griffin interrupts the moment and thank God he does. I release a breath I didn't know I was holding when she nods a yes and she and Griffin joke about something. I can't even hear what; I'm too busy giving myself a pep talk to get my shit together.

Something about her has me tongue tied. Could be the fact that I'm hard as a rock for her and it's a bit difficult to hide in these shorts. I think of everything and anything to rectify that situation.

Other than my lack of a brain when she's around me, everything is easygoing. The conversation flows and I was right to think Griffin would only put Magnolia at ease.

Something's still off, though. Every so often she looks at me from the corner of her eye and I don't know what she's searching for, but whatever it is, she isn't finding it if the look on her gorgeous face is anything to go by.

"You all right?" I ask her when I catch her doing it again.

"Yeah, it's just ..."

I don't speak up when she hesitates. I wait for her to get whatever it is off her chest. She didn't tell me the other night whatever it was that bothered her. Might as well get it over with now that the awkwardness is gone. Well, her awkwardness. I'm obviously still working on mine.

"It looked like just from a distance, you know … like you might be having a hard morning or something?"

"What do you mean?" A deep crease settles in my forehead.

"This morning … I might have been watching you for a bit … before I got on the boat."

A gruff chuckle leaves me. "I'm fine," I answer with the lie, pretending like I don't know what she's talking about even though I know damn well she must've seen me when I was thinking of Gramps. I can barely get a grip on the easy stuff. Heavy shit can wait till another day.

Quick to change the subject back to something we both enjoy, I tell her, "I see why you love it here."

"Yeah, the ocean, the sun … the town's not too bad either."

I join her when she laughs although I pick up on the dampened tone when she brings up the town.

"Small towns can be rough from what I've heard."

"Every place has its ups and downs but I do love it here."

"You going to live here forever?"

"Well, I haven't thought about 'forever' yet. It's hard with—" She stops speaking abruptly but her mouth stays parted, like she realized she was going to say something she doesn't want to.

"Hard with what?"

"With what happened a few years back. I didn't tell you ... I left that morning, the morning after we met because I had a family emergency and it turned into the worst time of my life."

"You want to talk about it?"

"No ... if that's okay with you?"

Shrugging to keep it casual I tell her, "I'm happy to talk about whatever you want."

"You could find out easily, though. You really could find out everything." Like something's dawned on her.

"Find out what?"

"Anything really. The town likes to gossip and knows everything." She gets her confidence back and grabs a drink from the cooler. It takes a moment, and all the while I can practically see the wheels turning in her head. "So what have you heard about me?"

I can feel Griffin watching us, as if he's a lifeguard on duty and he just knows I'm going to drown out at the helm with her. "I don't want to hear what the town's got to say, to be honest."

"So you haven't heard anything?" she asks like she doesn't believe me.

"Nope."

"I feel like this isn't second date talk." Griffin interrupts us, taking up the space to my right, with Magnolia still to my left. I'm tempted to kick his ass overboard.

He continues, "What is second date talk is asking about friends. Like if your friend Renee is single and if she'd like to come sailing ... or what her thing is?"

I'm so happy I brought a fifth wheel ...

Magnolia laughs and it's the sweetest sound. "I invited her but she had to decline unfortunately."

"Ah well," Griffin says, playing it off well, "maybe next time then." It's obvious as all hell that he's giving us space when he heads to the bow of the ship, looking out over the water as if there's something to see there. The shoreline does look gorgeous, I'll give him that.

"You want kids?" Magnolia asks me out of nowhere.

I can't help but to think about her daughter. I almost bring her up, but I bite my tongue instead and think of how to answer her. "I do. I want a big family."

"How big?" she asks and Griffin's comment about appropriate second date talk comes to mind, but this isn't really our second date.

"That would depend on a lot of things, I think. I'm an only child and I know I want at least two, maybe three ... maybe more."

She only nods, sipping her beer and staring out at the water.

I would ask her how many she wants, but she scoots closer to me, close enough that her forearm touches mine and I'm too busy enjoying the moment to break it up with questions that won't change a damn thing about what I want from her.

There's something here and I just need to kiss her. She'll feel it all too, as soon as she lets me kiss her.

CHAPTER 13

MAGNOLIA

"I've got a little burn, but it'll tan over."

Back at the pier, our legs dangle over the ledge. The trees behind us offer a bit of much-needed shade after half a day on the boat.

I need a nap after spending all day soaking in the sun. More than that, I need Brody to kiss me. All the little touches have added up. A girl can only take so much.

"Not as bad as Griffin's," Brody says with a smirk. His friend is going to be hurting, that's for certain.

"Where'd he go?" I say, already turning around to see if I can spot him. The piña colada water ice drips out just slightly from the bottom of the paper cone in my hand, so I tilt it back as I search him out, gathering the last of the frozen treat.

"He's heading out to get dinner with his family, I think."

I've learned a number of things in the last few hours. More than half were about Griffin. The man can talk and Brody was more quiet than anything. Observing, scooting closer to me and then I did the same.

It's probably a good thing Griffin was on that boat with us, to be honest.

"Now we're all alone," Brody practically hums, bumping his shoulder against mine and I have to laugh. There are about a dozen people behind us at the Ice Shack. Alone, we are not.

"You're funny," I say as I stand to chuck the paper cone in the nearby trash can.

"And you're cute," Brody calls out. He's got a sun-kissed tan now that completes his charming good boy, yet blue-collar look. If his hair was longer and his body leaner, he could be a surfer. But with his ruggedness and broad shoulders, and his hair cropped back ... he's all man candy to me.

He's handsome. My kind of handsome. The little flip my heart does tells me it agrees with me.

I keep the comment to myself but the smile on my face won't quit, so I bite down on my bottom lip as I join him again, legs hanging over the water, even as I lean back to lie on the wooden posts of the pier.

I could stay here forever, staring up at his blue eyes as he peers down at me like he has something on his mind. He's practically done it all day. Testing his words before he says them. He's careful with me.

"Maybe you're cute too," I whisper, feeling the warmth over my body spread deeper and flow through every inch of me.

It's a scary feeling, like playing with fire.

With his head thrown back, all I can do is watch the ripple of the muscles in his arms as he covers his face with both hands and groans.

"What?" I ask. His simple white T-shirt stretches over his shoulders as he faces me to confess, "You have no idea what I want to do to you right now."

My breath leaves me in a single quick exhale. "Oh yeah?" I whisper and I don't know how I can even talk right now. "What's that?"

"I want to lean down and kiss you. Put my hand right on those curves of yours. And kiss you in front of all these people in a town that likes to talk."

His gaze lingers on my waist before drifting back up to mine. All I can feel is the thump of my racing heart, begging him to do just that.

"You should do it," I murmur and shock widens my eyes at my own admission.

His lips hit me first. Soft but strong, taking a kiss much bolder and sweeter than the peck the other night. His tongue sweeps along the seam of my lips, begging for entry. All the while my blood heats and my pulse races. What was I thinking?

What am I thinking now, as I do what I want and not what I should, parting my lips and deepening the kiss. The act grants me a soft groan of approval from the man hovering above me, his fingers gripping my hips harder and pinning me down.

Stop. Stop! You haven't told him.

The small voice in the back of my head is meager but desperate. I pull back with an image of Bridget in my mind. It holds me back from drifting above in a hot air balloon and instead the reality anchors me back down to reality.

Breathe.

I focus on breathing as I sit up and Brody pulls away. I don't think he can tell how freaked out I am. No, no, I don't know if he can tell or not.

I'm only in my midtwenties and this seems exactly like something I should do ... but not with a daughter at home and secrets that are bound to ruin it all.

As I sit up, I can feel those blue eyes on me, once again observing and wondering, but holding back. If he can tell what I'm feeling, he must think I'm hot and cold. It's not fair to him.

Tell him. Just tell him.

"Brody," I start to say and he must hear the sudden panic in my tone, because he cuts me off.

"Today went perfectly, I think." It's all he says, but his gaze is soft as he leans closer, pecking my cheek and then he stares off into the water.

It's so obvious to me in this moment how much I'm falling for him. He's sweeter than I remember. He's gentler than what I used to hold on to.

I have to tell him. He's careful with me, and I'm nothing but reckless.

My lips part and I swear I'm going to tell him. Just blurt it out and rip the bandage off but his phone rings.

Saved by the ringtone.

"One sec," he tells me and answers it. It seems like a business call with how often he says yeah and that's fine.

Every second that passes gets me more nervous but I hold on to what I have to do. I need to tell him before this goes any further. He deserves to know.

Picking at some nonexistent fuzz on my cover-up, I wait for him to say goodbye.

The second he does, he speaks first. "I have to get going. You want me to drive you back?"

Tell him, tell him, I will myself but instead all I say is, "I drove."

"Right," he says then shakes his head in a boyish way but the smile that slips onto his lips is all charming man. "I knew that."

The little voice is quiet and so are both of us. He leans in again, his hand cupping the back of my head to give me a sweet goodbye kiss, but when he pulls away, he nips my bottom lip. A shy laugh slips out from me.

I'm still looking down at the worn wood of the pier, disappointed with myself but unable to stop myself from falling.

His thumb on my chin is what forces me to meet his ever-questioning gaze. "I'll text you tonight?" He says the statement like it's a question and all I can do is nod.

With his hand outstretched, he attempts to help me up but I tell him I'm going to stay here another minute. All I'm left with is a salty breeze and an achy heart. And guilt. So much guilt.

When I tell him now, I already know he's going to ask why I didn't tell him sooner.

And it's because I'm selfish, because I want to feel this warmth of falling for him again. I want to feel wanted. It's not until after he's already gone that I let the tears slip out. This is something I know I can never have. And Bridget deserves better.

The keys jingle in my hand and my flip-flops slap on the sidewalk as I make my way up to my front door. I'm so focused on the plan I laid out that I don't notice anyone's there waiting for me on the wicker chair out front.

"The sun's kissing you more than I am." Robert's voice startles me and when I jump back with a gasp, he throws his hands up. With a charming smile on his lips, he huffs a laugh and apologizes. "Shit, I'm sorry, Mags," he says and the laugh lingers in his voice.

With a hand placed over my racing heart, I smile back at him. "I didn't see you there."

"I can tell," he jokes and the air is easy between us.

"I have to run but I just wanted to drop this off for Bridget," he tells me and holds out a stuffed bear. There's obviously something hard in the ears and when he squeezes it the ears spin.

"Ooh, it's … oh what's it called?"

"Buzzy the Bear." He shrugs and hands it to me. It's not wrapped and still has the tag on it. He never wraps them, never tells Bridget the toys are from him. They're for me to give to her because he knows how much I struggle. It's hard to do anything really on a single income in this town. If guilt could kill someone, I'd be struck dead here on my front porch. Instead my fingers just go numb and my throat tight.

"Thanks," I say and have to clear my throat, holding the bear with both hands. "They have one at daycare and she threw a fit the other day when she couldn't take the darn thing home."

"I know … I heard. She's coming along good with the transition; little social butterfly."

An unwarranted huff leaves me. "Of course you heard. Is there anything this town doesn't talk about?" My ears burn at the rhetorical question, knowing that kiss on the pier is going to make its rounds.

"I just asked Trent how she was doing is all," Robert replies and a certain look flashes in his eyes. Maybe it's doubt, but possibly regret.

Pushing the hair out of my face, I clear my head and apologize. "Sorry, I just ... long day." The excuse is a pathetic one, but it works to ease the worry from his face.

"You been crying?" he asks and a different look replaces the one that was just there.

"No," I lie and his head tilts in an instant.

"It's not a problem. Just ... just life."

"You need me to do anything?" he asks and I struggle to swallow the lump in my throat.

"You don't need to be my hero," I answer with something I've said a dozen times before. When he slips his hand into his pocket to grab his keys, he replies with what he's said a dozen times too. "Maybe I want to be your hero."

I can only smile when he leaves a quick kiss on my cheek. The opposite one to where Brody kissed me. My words and every confession threaten to strangle me.

What am I doing?

"See you soon?" he asks and he sounds hopeful. It's different from usual.

"Yeah, of course," I answer him and watch the man I once loved with everything in me leave. A man who's protected me and helped me when he didn't have to.

If this were another life, today would have been a fairytale. Brody would be my fairytale prince. But this is real life and mine doesn't fit with his. Instead, I cry myself to sleep, and promise myself that I'll tell both of them tomorrow. I have to make the promise over and over again just so I can fall asleep, Brody's text going unread on my phone.

THREE YEARS AGO

"I hate teething," I say and the groan that accompanies my statement comes complete with my eyes closed and a hand over my face as Robert comes in through the front door. Slowly opening them, I speak over Bridget's wail. "I hate it more than I hate heartburn."

Seriously, I'd take that awful pregnancy heartburn and a bottle of Tums over my baby girl's teeth coming in. My right leg constantly bounces with her settled on my thigh and clinging to my arm.

At the sight of Robert, she cries louder, as if I've been unable to hear her all night and only he can save her.

The prick at the back of my eyes comes back. "I don't know what to do," I admit to him.

"Give her here, maybe I can calm her down," he offers and I give her up.

"Orajel," I start to rattle off, "strips of frozen waffles …"

"You've got all the teething toys out," Robert says and all of the primary- and pastel-colored rubbery toys on the seat next to me are evidence of that.

"She doesn't like them."

"What about … a cold rag?" he asks and I remember I threw one in the freezer last week. It's just a little washcloth, dipped in water and frozen. Please, Lord, let that be my lifesaver because I can't take much more of this.

Hustling to the freezer, I snag it and toss it to him. He catches it with one hand and offers it to a screaming Bridget who arches her back with complete distaste.

My heart plummets but Robert assures me, "Give me five."

Five minutes. He can have all the five minutes he needs.

"Teething is a bitch," I say as I rub my eyes and make my way back to the kitchen. With the perfectly good pan of untouched lasagna staring back at me from the stovetop, I realize I haven't even eaten dinner. How is it already nine at night?

"Ooh, shots fired."

"What?"

"You must be really worked up," he tells me, swinging little Bridget to and fro in large circles back and forth, "You're cussing like a sailor."

The flame of a blush brightens my cheeks. "Oh, hush," I say, waving him off although he's right. I don't like cussing. Doesn't mean I don't do it my head, though; I was just raised not to.

I mutter under my breath as I open the top of the lasagna and touch it only to find it cold, "Teething is a bitch, though."

It's at that thought I realize she's not crying anymore. Holding my breath, I peek over the threshold and watch Robert still swinging Bridgey, but now she's got both of her hands on the rag, gnawing away.

"Yesssss." My hiss of happiness makes Robert laugh and I still in my victory crouch, waiting to make sure his laugh didn't disturb her.

After a solid five seconds, I'm convinced it didn't and more grateful than Robert will ever know.

Sometimes a mom just needs a break.

"You are my hero," I whisper, my hands in a prayer position.

"I'm glad you texted me," he says, slowing down his swings to be more gentle.

As I'm wondering if she'll let me give her a bottle this time since she refused her last feeding, Robert suggests I go to bed.

"You look like you need some sleep," he adds.

The last thing I want to do after the day I've had is go to bed. I need a moment. I don't know how to describe it to him. Because he's right, I've barely slept the last two nights, but I just need to be ... to be me for a moment. And to know everything is all right.

Without answering him, I make a bottle and take a steadying breath.

"You're starting to resemble a raccoon," he jokes.

"They're my new favorite animal," I say, shaking the bottle with my finger on the nipple. When I get back to the living room, he's preparing to sit down with her and it makes me nervous.

"Pass it on over," he offers with his hand out. Bridget's still going to town on that little washcloth and that's when I realize I should prepare another.

Handing off the bottle, I practically run to the hall closet to find a clean washcloth and do with it just what I did with the other. Run it under the water, wring it out, and place it in my freezer.

My stomach rumbles, so after wiping off my hands on my pajama pants, I place the lasagna back in the oven.

"Did you eat?" I ask Robert, hopeful he didn't so I can pay him back with a meal at least.

"I could eat," he answers from the sofa, one hand on the bottle, the other slyly reaching for the remote. "Seriously, I can hang out with little miss until she sleeps if you want to sleep."

"I don't want to sleep, I just need a minute to decompress ..."

He shrugs. "Whatever you want to do. You still watch that one show?"

"I'm so far behind it's not even funny," I tell him and flop down next to him. It feels like it's well past midnight but it's not even close to being that late.

Silently, Robert finds the show and the next episode that hasn't been marked watched. I'm six behind. I let out a small hum of satisfaction, one not too unlike the little sounds of glee from my baby girl next to me.

The oven beeps a moment later, coming up to temperature and I almost get up before realizing it's not the timer. Five more minutes. My body feels heavier, finally resting.

"You don't know how thankful I am," I whisper to Robert, letting my cheek rest on the sofa.

A charming smirk lifts up his lips and he says, "I remember when Danielle had her little girl." Danielle's his cousin. "It can be rough at times, but it gets better."

My lids feel so heavy.

"Dinner and sleep?" Robert asks me and I humph in opposition to the suggestion of sleep. "I'm not going to bed just yet and you don't have to stay here."

"Yeah, okay," he answers with both humor and cockiness. I almost tell him I'm so grateful we're still friends, but then flashes of some of these nights come back, and I don't want to put the label of "friend" on it. Even if we don't say it, we're more than friends.

Even if no one knows and it's a secret ... it's more than that to me and I've never been more grateful to have him in my life.

CHAPTER 14

BRODY

"She likes you," Griffin comments when I glance at my phone again. He says it like I need to hear it. Raking his hand through his hair, he raises his brow and looks me dead in the eye wanting confirmation that I agree.

All he gets is a frustrated sigh. My gut instinct says she doesn't. No matter what I do, I can't shake that feeling.

Apparently unsatisfied with my silence, Griffin adds, "If she didn't like you, she wouldn't have said yes."

The iron legs of the chair on the side patio of Charlie's drag across the ground, scraping it as I lean back. A group of three women filter in through the small gate in the back. It's almost lunch hour and judging by their skirts and flowy blouses, they got out early to beat the crowd.

That's kind of the reason we're here too. I have a lunch date with Magnolia and she suggested this place—of all places.

Our date started five minutes ago and instead of Griffin getting up to offer Magnolia a seat and tell her he was just heading out, he's still here and I'm still tapping my fingers against the side of my phone, waiting for her.

"I'm getting mixed signals." Damn, it sucks to say it out loud. But days have passed with only a few texts exchanged and a lunch date made. She's barely said a word in all of that. She doesn't initiate contact; she's always late to reply. "I've never had this much trouble getting a woman to talk to me."

"You sound like a girl." His dismissive answer comes complete with the flip of the paperwork in his hands. It's what we need to fill out to file for the last license. It's already been submitted ... twice.

That's what I should be focused on. I didn't spend the last few years to waste it all by not paying attention.

The cold beer is at odds with the warm air. At least there's a breeze, though, with a touch of salt but it's fresh. Every morning I breathe in deep and love the air here.

I tell Griffin exactly what I told myself this morning, "I don't want to waste my time going after someone who isn't after me."

"Just have another drink." Griffin's comical irritation only makes me smirk at him.

"Another one?" The waitress pops her blond head out from the side door just then. Taking a look down at my beer glass, now empty, I have to admit she's damn good at her job.

"Please," I say, having to raise my voice just slightly to be heard. She nods, peers at Griffin and goes back inside without another word.

She knows I have someone else coming. I told her when she offered to take the menus since we weren't eating.

With a click of the side button, 11:53 stares back at me on the phone. Quarter to noon is when we were supposed to meet … eight minutes past. Maybe she's inside.

Griffin must know that I'm checking out the inside to see if she's there and not out here, because he comments, "Inside seating doesn't open until noon on the dot."

His voice is flat as is the expression he gives me.

"Just relax." Griffin's advice is mixed with the sound of a new beer thudding on the table in front of me. The waitress doesn't say a word and the only bit of her I see is her back as she rushes over to the table of the three women who sat at the table next to us.

She must know them well, judging by how she bends down with both palms on the table and the three women lean in.

It's getting easier to recognize some people around town. It really is a small place, which is crazy considering the location. If this town was on the East Coast, it'd be packed.

I watch the first woman readjust the cloth napkin on her

lap although she still seems attentive to whatever is being talked about. One of the women drops her mouth open to a perfect O with her eyes wide as another woman smacks the table and the whispers get louder.

I admit something that's been bugging me since the pier. "I'm not going to lie, a very big piece of me wants to know what people say about Magnolia."

My attention falls back to Griffin. With nothing but a single crease down the center of his forehead, his expression is discerning.

"What?"

"I already looked into that," he tells me. "If there's something you want to know ..." With his palm upturned and lying flat on the table, he waits.

"What'd they say about her being single? She is available, right?" I question him again. I know he said she was before and he's already nodding, confirming that she is.

"She's single. She went through a rough time right when she came back from college."

"But it's not because of me, right? You would have told me that."

Although it seems like he's holding back, he shakes his head and tells me, "She's a young girl who went through a hard time. Her father died; there was scandal with that. She told you that on the boat."

Feeling like an insecure prick, I take a swig of my beer. "It just feels like rejection. That's what this all feels like."

"Look, just get to know her. You like her. She likes you. The other stuff, no matter how big or small ... Talk to her. Ask her how late she's running if you want to know so bad."

Just as Griffin mutters under his breath, "It's not like you don't know where your phone is," the little gate to the patio opens with a creak, hushing everything else in my head.

There she is, in a yellow sundress that flows around her curves as the breeze blows by again.

Her eyes catch mine instantly and I force a smile to my lips. I don't realize I haven't breathed until Griffin stands, blocking my view of her.

As they exchange niceties, I get my shit together. What the hell is this woman doing to me?

"Was just heading out," he tells her and then raises his voice to add, "Have a nice lunch date, you two." His grin is wide as he heads out and Magnolia takes a seat in his former chair which he already pulled out for her.

"Hey beautiful," I say and the worried look on her beautiful face fades.

Brushing the locks away from her face, she lets out a small sigh and apologizes. "I had a meeting with my boss about an event coming up. I'm so sorry I'm late."

"It's fine," I tell her and even shrug like I wasn't sitting here worried.

"I don't make a habit of being late," she says sweetly and

focuses on the menu when the waitress gets to our table.

"You want your usual?" the waitress questions Magnolia and it takes her a long moment to shake her head. "I think just an iced tea and shrimp and spinach salad."

With a nod and a scribble in her pad, the waitress gives me her attention. I don't even know what I ordered, I just say the special. I knew half an hour ago what it was, though. I'm sure it'll be fine.

"How'd the meeting go?" I start with small talk, but all I can think about is that kiss on the pier. I really thought I had her after that kiss.

A stirring in my jeans makes me shift in my seat. Fuck, I know I wanted her after that kiss. I still do.

"It went well, just a lot of prep for an event because the guest list is so large."

"It's for a gala?" She already told me all about it this past weekend on the boat. I just don't get what happened between then and now. I remember Griffin's suggestion to ask her whatever's on my mind. Just to talk to her. But apparently I'm chickenshit.

"Yup," she says with a nod and the waitress appears from out of nowhere again, iced tea in hand which Magnolia accepts. She sips from the straw while holding it and then stirs a bit of sugar in it.

"Hey listen," I start, and shift again in the uncomfortable-ass chair, which is now way too fucking small for me. That's all I get out as the words slam themselves into the back of my throat and I glance to her right, remembering how she took off the first time I saw her here.

"Yeah?" she asks softly, carefully even. She pushes the iced tea away slightly before folding her hands in her lap. It's proper behavior maybe, but it doesn't feel right to me.

"Did something happen?" I say, shoving the words out there impatiently.

Her quizzical look in those striking blue eyes gets a follow-up from me. "Between the dock and now, I just get the feeling that maybe you aren't interested."

"What?" The nervous tucking of her hair behind her ear and the way she shifts in her chair are at odds with the nonchalant "what" she gives me. The surprise in her voice is enough to tell me I'm probably off base. Fucking hell. I don't know what to think.

"I really like you and I'm fine with taking things slow. I thought maybe the pier wasn't what I thought it was ... you don't seem to want to talk."

"I've just been really busy." Why does that sound like a lie to me? Staring into her eyes, she doesn't flinch or back down. Not for a good two seconds until she's forced to look away.

"You've been busy?"

She doesn't look back at me, just nods and takes a drink of the water on the table rather than her iced tea.

The uncomfortable squirm in my seat is confirmation

enough. Mixed signals. I think I'm going to change her name to that in my phone.

It's quiet for a long time and I would kick my own ass if I could for even bringing it up. I should know better than to take dating advice from Griffin.

"Why Rose?" I ask her to keep from going down this rabbit hole. Although the pit in my stomach only gets heavier remembering how all of it started with a lie years ago.

"What? ... Why the name Rose?" she says, figuring out the answer to her own question before I can clarify.

"Yeah," I answer her. "I was thinking about that the other night. I almost called you Rose on the dock."

"I wanted to be someone else when we met back then."

"I already knew that. I don't know why, though."

"Stupid reason. If I'd known what was coming, I wouldn't have been so messed up that night." Her response is cryptic until she takes a deep breath that makes her chest rise and fall and then looks back at me with a sad smile to add, "A boyfriend broke up with me."

She lets out a small huff of a laugh. The tense air seems to dissipate some when she apologizes for the second time since she sat down. "Sorry I lied to you."

There's nothing but sincerity in her eyes. "Don't be. I'm glad I met you that night."

There's a warmth that flows through me as her smile widens. "You have no idea how happy I am that I met you."

Her gaze falls to the table again when she adds, "It sucks how it ended, though."

"It didn't end yet." I have to correct her and the look she gives me back is a telling one. She's scared about something. Nothing changed between the pier and now. It hits me then. She ran the first time I saw her. There's a reason for it and didn't she want to tell me that before? "Whatever's on your mind, just get it out there. I can take it," I offer.

"It's not something so easy as to say it over lunch."

"Some things are better over dinner then?" It's a light joke. One that's followed by the undeniable pull of the connection and sexual tension that's always there between us.

"Promise you won't hate me after?" she whispers and her eyes shine with unshed tears.

"There's nothing—" I don't even get to finish my sentence before she takes a sharp inhale. Her gaze is glued to something—or someone—behind me.

A second passes, maybe only a fraction of a second but it's enough time that I look over my shoulder and see two men. One young, our age maybe, and the other older with similar features. I imagine they're related.

The guy who's my age I've seen before, but I can't place where. This town is small and everyone is starting to feel familiar. I turn back to Magnolia, slowly and carefully to see her pouty lips still parted and an uncomfortable pinch in her brow. With her wide eyes filled with worry, she offers an apology, her words clipped as she does. "I'm sorry."

"Mags?" the younger guy calls out and the air changes entirely.

"I have to—" she doesn't finish the thought before getting up from the table with the obvious intention of making her way to one of the two men behind us.

All I can think is that she's seeing him and they're a thing. That is the overwhelming instinct. That she's a cheater and I'm the other man. It's more than just disappointment that pangs in my chest.

"Look, if there's something you aren't telling me ..." I start to say and my words halt her even though I stay seated. "... I can take it if you just aren't interested." I swear if I move an inch, I won't be able to stop myself from following her.

She looks hurt, then I realize it's more than that. Shit. The way her expression falls, it's obvious my words crushed her. I feel the need to apologize but I don't have a chance.

"It's just a little complicated for me, Brody." Her words sound strangled and unlike the other times that telltale feeling of eyes watching us has crept up on me, Magnolia seems oblivious to it, lost in her own chaotic thoughts. "If I didn't want you, I would tell you. I just need ... I need a little time."

"I understand that, and—" She's already walking away before I can finish. Before I can tell her I'm sorry.

The other guests are quiet and I know they're watching. I replay the scene in my head and I wish I could rewind, be less

... anxious and pushy with her. Is that what I was? She's got me so turned around I don't know what I'm even doing anymore.

Other than playing the part of a fool. There's something she's not telling me and I think it has to do with whomever she saw just then. It feels like everyone around me already knows. The waitress is polite enough to ask if I just want the check when she comes out. And kind enough not to mention the fact that my date just took off.

She's not polite enough to gossip a bit, though, and tell me the guy Magnolia spotted is some dude named Robert and that they used to be a thing.

"Used to?" I press her and the blond waitress shrugs, not wanting to give me any more information.

The questions pile up and as I sit there, waiting on the bill and our lunches the waitress offered to box up for me, not that I'm in the mood for eating any of it, I text Griffin.

I thought the town said she's single. That's what you told me. But it doesn't look that way.

His response is telling: There might be a complication ... or two.

Chapter 15

Magnolia
A little over two years ago...

Knock, knock, knock. The knocking at the front door is hesitant. My tired eyes lift from the open laptop I've been staring at for hours and travel to the front door. As I rise up off the sofa, I peek down the hall. Bridget should be sound asleep for the night; she's been sleeping so well recently, which has been a blessing. Still, I hold my breath as I tiptoe to the front door wondering who's knocking at nine o'clock at night.

It can only be Robert or Renee, but they wouldn't knock.

I have to stand on my tiptoes to peek through the peephole and see Robert combing his hand through his dirty blond hair as he glances behind him.

My heart does a little flutter, but it's an odd one. Not one filled with the kind of anticipation I'm used to feeling when I see him.

Probably because his expression holds a hint of concern and he didn't text before dropping by. As the lock slides from the bolt, I'm very well aware that he would have normally texted beforehand.

The door creaks open and instantly the chill of the sea breeze air clings to my bare shoulders which were covered by the blanket only a moment ago.

"Hey, you okay?" I ask instantly and step back, wanting more of the heat of my apartment over the crisp autumn air. "You didn't text," I say, adding the explanation as Robert steps in, closing the door and apologizing at the same time.

"Sorry," he says as he loosens the tie around his neck and unbuttons the top button of his shirt. It's a simple white button-up but it's wrinkled, probably from sitting in meetings all day. The black dress pants and leather belt complete the new look he's had since he started working at Town Hall.

"It's my dad," he starts, flopping down on the sofa. Dead smack in the center of it, which is his spot.

I've always had a hard time controlling my expression, mostly because of my rebellious brows. So when they quirk up, the left one arched as if to respond, "Your dad? Seriously?" Robert only laughs and pats the right cushion next to him. My spot. It boasts the still-warm blanket that I cuddle into as I sit beside him. My laptop is open on the coffee table and

Robert gets a peek.

"You working on websites now?" he asks.

"Well no, just making notes for the guy who does ... we need a lot of plugins added so we can do more with it."

He hums and nods. I don't let him off the hook so easily, saying, "It's just a side project for the gallery. What's going on with your dad?"

A yawn sneaks out after the words leave my mouth, though. It's so late.

"I shouldn't have come," Robert says with a groan, letting his head fall back. "I'm sorry," he tells me again and I smack his arm playfully.

"Quit it, and spit it out."

"He wants me to have a date for the event this weekend."

My caged heart protests at the word date but I remain silent.

"He wants me to bring someone, like as a guest to it."

"Okay," I say, playing dumb, barely responding at all as I lean forward and close the laptop.

"I know we aren't a thing and he said he told the governor I'd go with his niece who's in town ... looking at colleges," he adds absently as I let what he's saying sink in.

"Okay, so what's the problem?" I ask, playing it cool, ignoring every little emotion that feels like a thousand tiny pinpricks along my skin. I think I might even be sick just thinking about him with some pretty little thing on his arm at whatever fancy event is this weekend. I think it's a charity for the library opening. This last week has been crazy with work and Bridget and I don't remember what it was that he told me.

"So I think I ... I am going with her ..." His statement is uttered haltingly but his baby blue eyes never stop peering into mine. I'm the one who looks away.

"Okay, and you told your dad yes?" I ask him, my heart already breaking in half. We're only friends, I remind myself. This was bound to happen. We had a good run ... the thought lingers on the tip of my tongue.

"I didn't answer him. I left."

"Oh, okay."

"Do you want me to tell him no?" he asks me. Like his life decisions should be in my hands.

"Why would I want that?" I question him back even though my throat feels suddenly so much smaller than it should. Tighter and dry.

"I don't want you to be upset if I—"

"We're just friends," I say, cutting him off and reach forward for my laptop. "It's totally fine," I add with as upbeat a tone as possible. "If you really like her, though—"

"I don't even know her," he blurts out, interrupting me and he immediately sounds defensive, like it's a fight. I don't want to fight with him. I don't want to lose him. I can't imagine either of those possibilities right now so I shush him and look him dead in the eye when I tell him, "Seriously, Robert. It's fine. We're just friends and I'm not upset."

"Yeah," he answers, his gaze falling from mine to the floor, "just friends."

PRESENT DAY

It's taking everything in me not to cry right now. The radio is barely on, but it's on nonetheless, playing a love song and mocking me as I lean back in the driver's seat and focus on taking deep breaths. The keys are still in the ignition even though the car is parked in my designated spot for the development.

I didn't tell my boss, Mandy, that I locked up shop for the day and came right home. I have no idea what she'll do or say when she finds out but I imagine I can't confess to her and that she'll understand. I saw a man who I loved and have been sleeping with for years while on a date with a man who might be the father of my child. I haven't told either of them so I had to get the hell out of there before my little girl comes home so I can try to pull myself together.

Yeah, I can't do that. Mandy doesn't care about the mess I created. And yet, I did it anyway and I'm already coming up with another lie to add onto the pile. This one is the first for my boss: I felt absolutely ill out of nowhere and I had to go home. I suppose it's not a complete lie. I could throw up right now just thinking about the look on Robert's face when he saw me with Brody.

For being such a bad liar, I sure have told a lot of them to Brody.

I imagine what would have happened had I stayed seated there and a soap opera plays out in my head. Entertainment for the entire town.

It still hurts. It all hurts right now. Brody sees right through me. He sees that I'm a liar. I could see it in his eyes and it freaking hurts but that's what I deserve, isn't it? All these lies piling up. White lie or not. All I could think when he looked at me, even now when I close my eyes and see his handsome smile curve down, is: he's never going to believe me about Bridget. And if he does, he'll never forgive me.

The soap opera would have ended with me in tears and a broken heart. I knew it, sitting there and glancing between the two men. I can take my karma, and I will. Just not in front of everyone else. Please, whoever is up there, listening to this prayer, please let me go through it without an audience this time. Please. I'll take what's coming to me, but I just don't want everyone to see my heartbreak again.

The console clicks as I open it, rummaging through the clutter of old sunglasses and sunblock for a napkin. I just need something to dab at the corner of my eyes in the rearview mirror.

I'm so caught up with just breathing and gathering my

thoughts that I don't hear the heavy thud of a car door beyond my pathetic sniffle.

It's not until he calls my name that I'm aware there's anyone outside my car door.

"Mags, please." My chest tightens, painfully so. "Mags." The way he says my name cuts through me, like he's sad for me, drawing it out and before I can respond, my door is opened.

"I need a minute, Robert." It's all I can get out, balling up the napkin, and struggling with my seat belt. He was halfway crouched down to meet me at eye level but my words bring him to a halt. He takes a single step back even though the door is still open and his hand is on top of it.

"Did he hurt you?"

"What?" With the keys still in the ignition, the car scolds me, but yells nearly as loudly as my inner thoughts do to confess to Robert, right now. "Hurt me?" My brow scrunches as I rip the keys out of the ignition and grab my purse off the passenger seat.

Robert takes another half step back so I can get the heck out of the hot car. Deep breaths. "No, he didn't hurt me."

I can barely look Robert in the eyes. When I do, there's confusion, but mostly hurt. He knows darn well I was on a date. He's never seen me with another man. Not once. The next deep breath is a torturous one as I shut the door to my car and make my way up the stairs. With every click of my heels there's a clack of his shoes following me across the pavement.

It's only when I get to my door, the key in the lock ready to turn, that Robert speaks again, "I didn't know you were interested in seeing someone."

I'm frozen where I am, my back to him and my eyes closed. I have to lean forward and rest my forehead against the door when he adds, "In fact, you said the opposite."

It's not a lie. But it's not like he was asking me out when I told him that and it was years ago. He was seeing someone. That's why the conversation came up.

He continues, "You said you didn't want anyone."

I said it to make him feel better. I remember the conversation all too well. One more lie to add to my pile. Maybe I've always been a liar and I just didn't see it until now.

"At the time I didn't," I say, adding another lie to the pile. What's one more, at this point? I wanted him. I wanted Robert to choose me to take to whatever event it was. Not some governor's niece. But between myself and the woman he told me about ... there was no chance he would take me. I knew what we were and I came to terms with it.

With his tall frame standing only feet from me, it's easy to see how his posture deflates. It's everything about him that tells me his heart is shredded.

Why does it hurt as much as it does? It shouldn't. But looking at Robert, it kills me to tell him anything I'm feeling inside. It hasn't felt like this in years. It's always been easy. Both of us finding comfort in one another.

"I don't know what I want," I say, finally speaking some truth.

His voice is drenched with wretched emotion as he says, "I've been with you from the very beginning, Mags."

The way he says my name is pleading.

"I want to take you out."

"Rob—" He cuts me off as I step forward, feeling the pull of two incompatible wants in my life.

"Just a date," he assures me, his hands raised in defeat.

"You sure you want to be seen with me?" The joke I've made for years makes my voice tight and my eyes prick with tears.

Robert is softer, sweeter when he takes my hands in his. This man and Brody are the only two men I've ever been with and I've only let myself fall in love with one. Fair enough, though, only one has broken my heart.

It takes everything in me to rip my hands away from his and get the confession out there. The weight of it is destroying me.

"I have to tell you something. Before you tell me you want me. Brody ... the guy I was with ..." The prick at the back of my eyes burns and I struggle to say anything without fear of losing it.

"Mags," he says and Robert's consoling voice is accompanied by his arms wrapping around me. He pulls me into his chest and holds me. He always has. Every time I come so close to breaking, this man has been here for me.

He whispers in my hair, "Whatever it is, you can tell me."

He kisses the top of my head. "I will still love you. You know I'll always love you."

First I cry, and I hate myself for it. I don't even know why I'm crying.

But then I tell him everything. I don't skip a single detail from four years ago, up till the moment we got here.

CHAPTER 16

BRODY

I take a deep breath in as I flip the dark wood coffee table over. It takes a grunt and a heave; the driftwood is heavier than it looks. The breeze blows through the small three-bedroom apartment, carrying the scent of the ocean with it, and I have to wipe my brow as I look down at the last piece of furniture put into place.

"It's still a man cave."

"Good, because that's what I was going for," I tell Griffin. With my shirt off, a thin sheen of sweat along my shoulders and the drill at my feet, it's obvious I've been working my ass off to get this place together. One thud is followed by another as Griffin plants his feet on the new coffee table, determined to already make an ass groove in the corner of the dark blue sectional I put together yesterday.

I don't say a damn word. I've barely said anything since three days ago when Magnolia said she needed time and then Griffin filled me in on why.

Fuck buddies or old flames, I don't know which exactly. All I know is that the girl I'm after has something going on with another man. Or did. I saw all the signs; I knew it deep down, and yet ...

"No more boxes," Griffin says absently, his voice just a tad louder than the constant clicking on the laptop balanced on his thighs.

"No more boxes," I repeat with a long exhale and make my way to the fridge for a beer, only to find it empty.

I check my phone again and stare at the text she sent after our so-called date: Hey, can we talk?

I didn't respond and I don't intend to. If she's going to write me off for some other guy, she can do it to my face. Maybe it's pride. Maybe I'm just pissed. Either way, I'm not letting her off easy.

"So what are you going to do now?" Griffin asks, not lifting his gaze from the computer screen. He's working on the website page, the online store and partners for retail. So I can't blame him for sitting his ass down and not doing a damn thing to help me furnish this place.

There's no more furniture to put together. No more

focusing on working a screwdriver or drill and not thinking about the woman who's under my skin.

"Shower," I answer easily enough and then lean against the countertop, taking a look around the place. It's minimal with dark woods, but light and bright white accents. It's airy and reminds me of the shore most of all. Which, I remind myself, is the entire reason I'm here.

Not for Rose or Magnolia, or whoever this woman wants to be.

Even if thoughts of her lips keep me up at night. Even if I can't help but want to rewind every moment we've had together so I can say the right things and end each night with a kiss like the one we had on the pier.

"You keep sighing like that and someone's going think you're depressed," Griffin says, mocking me from across the open living space. All I can do is give him a scowl in return but he doesn't see since he still hasn't looked up.

I crack my neck to the left and right and make my way around the counter to go shower and get my shit together.

"So she may have had a low-key thing with a guy. Maybe ... it's just a rumor."

I don't bother answering Griffin, I don't even halt my steps. The truth is it's not just a rumor when she's out with me but leaves the second she sees him. That's not fucking gossip; that's reality.

"You should just ask her," Griffin calls out as I walk down

the narrow hallway to the master suite. Again I don't answer him but I at least agree with that sentiment.

Shower. And then I'm damn well going to see her, talk to her and ask her if she's got anything to hide. If I could get her out of my head, I wouldn't bother.

But I can't and what's worse, is that I don't want her out of my head.

The ring that comes with the door to the gallery swinging open is followed by a "Welcome!" and then "I'll be with you in just one moment" from somewhere in the back right corner. It sounds like Magnolia is rearranging a piece or two with her back to the door. Her smile's bright and wide, looking gorgeous on her sun-kissed skin paired with a pale blue dress that has buttons all the way down the front of it.

Of course, it fades when she sees who it is who walked into her gallery. Her eyes grow a little wider, and I'd feel like shit if they didn't flash with something that looked like relief and her chest didn't flush all the way to her cheeks. If she didn't stand there looking back at me like I just stole her last breath.

Yeah, I'd feel like shit if our gazes weren't locked with something that seemed an awful lot like hope.

"You look beautiful." I can't help but to tell her.

"You always say that," she says then blushes deeper and

the smile comes back, although not full force.

I shrug. "You always look beautiful."

Tucking her hair behind her ear, she avoids my gaze as she tells me thank you beneath her breath and strides through the displays at a leisurely pace to the counter. Her on one side, me on the other.

When she finally peeks up at me, her forearms resting on the counter so she's leaning closer to me, I can see the desperation, the want, the longing in her doe eyes.

"You didn't text me back," she says, her voice soft and knowing.

"No, I didn't."

"So what are you doing in here?" Her voice is soft and velvetlike, but there's a sadness still present.

"You wanted to talk and I thought we should."

With a nod, she murmurs, "Right." Ripping her gaze from mine, she stands taller as a crease mars her forehead. "I have some things that I think you should know." She clears her throat and it's obvious she's uncomfortable.

"Is Robert one of those things?" I get right to the point, tired of this bullshit. "Because I don't really care if you had something before with him. If it's over, it's over. I give a shit that you up and leave me when you see him, though."

"He didn't know and—"

"Didn't know what?" I ask to clarify but hate that I cut her off when she's finally telling me what the hell is going on.

"That I was ..."

"That you were seeing me?"

"That I was seeing anyone. You don't understand." Frustration brings her hands to her hair and she takes a deep breath. I wait as she appears to start to say something but then takes another deep breath first.

"He helped me through a lot when I had no one. I owe him a lot and a big part of me loves him still. So I didn't want him to find out that I was seeing someone by literally walking in on a date."

"Do you still love him?"

"Not like that. I haven't loved him like that in a long time, but I don't want to hurt him." Her confession is earnest and she never breaks our gaze. Swallowing thickly, I let her confession settle before asking, "What do you want to do?"

Her gaze darts away from me and she hesitates.

"No more lies." I lay down the one thing I really need from her. No more hiding shit from me. It's driving me crazy. She's driving me damn near insane.

Her words are tight and her doe eyes pleading for understanding. "There's one more thing," she practically whispers.

The daughter. I already know she's got a kid. "Griffin told me you have a daughter."

"What else did he tell you?"

"The father's not in the picture, but it seems like Robert is the father to a number of people."

"Is that ..." Turmoil rolls through her after she trails off and I hate the tension in her body. She struggles to keep herself poised. With her eyes closed and her expression crumpled, I know the truth about her situation is tearing her apart. So I speak up, hating that whatever happened is killing her like it is.

"A problem for me? No." She doesn't react and I take a step forward, telling her every truth I have. "I want you and I told you I wanted a fair shot. You told him about me?" Adrenaline rushes through me at the thought of him being an obstacle because of a town rumor.

"Yes." There's not a single hint of hesitation in the answer but she still hasn't opened her eyes.

"Good. I just want to kiss you." I don't know that I've ever spoken a more honest statement. When she doesn't respond, still appearing trapped in the uncomfortable conversation, I lean forward against the counter and whisper, the tip of my nose close to hers, "I just want to kiss you, Magnolia."

Her lips part once but there are no words. Maybe she's not used to the bluntness. Maybe she thought having a daughter would send me packing.

"It hasn't been this hard for me to get a kiss in a long time ... probably since I met this girl at a bar named Rose. Took hours of convincing back then," I joke, attempting to lighten the mood. Her beautiful blue eyes open slowly but she doesn't budge.

Her expression softens but when she swallows, her throat tightens.

"I just want to kiss you," I repeat.

"Please," she pleads with me but I don't know what for.

"Please what? Tell me what you want," I say, pushing her for more.

"Please kiss me." Her voice is begging and I'm more than relieved to oblige, leaning over the counter with my hand gripping the back of her neck. It's a desperate, deep kiss that steals the tension, shattering it when her lips crack against mine.

If it was sparks I felt on the pier, as I did at the bar that night years ago, right here, right now, those sparks just burst into flames. Her lips part and I deepen the kiss, my hands moving lower.

Fumbling in between the heated kiss, she leads me back to the corner of the gallery. My body's pressed against hers, caging her in. Needing to breathe, she breaks the kiss but I can't. Not with the way her fingers dig into my shoulders like she needs me to stay right there with her. Nibbling down her neck, I let the memories of years ago wash over me and mix with the here and now.

A soft moan escapes her lips and my need turns primal. "I want you," I groan against the curve of her neck. This woman makes me want, she's a beautiful tease, but there's a softness and sweetness to her that makes the longing deeper and something more.

"I can't," she says in a breathy voice, calming herself with deeper breaths and finally loosening her grip on me.

"You worried someone's going to see?" I ask and glance over my shoulder. With my head spinning, and all the blood in my body nowhere near my brain, I come to the very obvious realization that this woman doesn't want to be fucked in her place of work.

Both of us still catching our breath, she answers me, "I haven't dated in a long time." The cords of her neck tense as she swallows then adds, "It's a small town and I already have scandal all over me. I don't really want any more."

"Kissing me would be scandalous?" I offer her an asymmetric grin and nudge my nose against hers.

Even though it lightens the tension, she's adamant. "We were doing a little more than kissing."

"I know," I tell her, "I get it."

There's a look in her eyes, like there's something else, but I tell her the one thing I decided, "If you want to kiss me, then kiss me."

She leans forward and plants a chaste kiss on my lips, this time molding her lips to mine a little more, and then gives me another, deepening it.

If she just keeps kissing me, there won't be any problems. Robert can fuck off now that there are no secrets between us.

CHAPTER 17

MAGNOLIA

"I am complete chicken poo." The theme song to Bridget's favorite show fills the living room. She's plopped cross-legged on the ottoman with mac and cheese on a little pink plate. Well ... there's some remnants of cheese left. I'm surprised my little girl didn't lick the plate she ate it so fast.

"It's ridiculous. I am an emotional wreck, for one, and chicken poo on top of that." I cannot believe I told Robert but not Brody. I just ... I just wanted him to kiss me again and I'm so afraid that he's never going to kiss me again.

"Chicken poo isn't quite what I'd call you." Renee says each word slowly, carefully, testing them out. One would think she's trying to comfort me, but knowing her she's trying to twist the words to come up with some sort of teasing joke to make me laugh. She bugged me for every sordid detail. So the moment I locked up at work and came home, Renee was on me. As if I wouldn't tell her anyway. She's the first and only person I texted.

She already knew he'd come to the shop, though. Apparently "the handsome young bachelor" is the talk of the town. And the town knows he's got an interest in me. I'm pretty sure the second part of the rumor going around is completely made up. The part about Brody and Robert hating one another. They don't even know each other.

I didn't bother to ask Renee if the town approves when she told me what was going around; I couldn't care less if they do.

Tossing a little pink unicorn into the air and letting out a deep exhale, I say, "He already had to deal with Robert and I still don't know how he found out about that."

"Maybe you freaking out because Robert looked your way was a clue?" Renee's voice is mocking as is her raised brow. "Like, just a tiny little clue?"

"A clue!" Bridget chimes in and gets both of our gazes to the back of her unmoving head. Her cute little locks bounce as she sways to the show.

"Is she listening?" Renee whispers.

"She's a three-year-old ... she's always listening. With her little bat-like sonar hearing," I whisper back.

Renee got all the good details first. The part about how

he confronted me and kissed me and got me all hot and bothered. And now we're stuck on the other part that goes hand in hand with that. The part where I probably should have told him my little girl is potentially his when I had the chance. Well, shoot.

A vibration on the coffee table alerts me to a text and I don't miss that Renee scoots closer to me from the plush chair she claimed as "her spot" when I first bought it. "Is it him?"

"You are worse than Miss Jones," I say, pretending to scold her as I guard the phone from her prying eyes.

"Pfft," is all I get in return as she sits back in the chair.

I really like kissing you.

A smile pulls my lips up and there's a warmth in my chest as I stare at the phone screen, both my hands wrapped around it.

My head falls back against the pillow and that's when Renee says, "It is him, and you're all gooey inside."

I like kissing you too.

"So what's the plan?" Renee asks and my sweet little innocent bubble pops. That's exactly what it feels like. When I'm with him, we're in our own little world where everything is perfect and all that matters are the butterflies in the pit of my belly.

And then my bubble pops. Just like it did now, right in time with the show ending on the television.

Clicking the power button, the screen goes black and Bridget yelps in protest. "Heyyyy!"

"Bedtime, little miss," I tell her and toss both the remote

and my phone on the ottoman.

Renee grabs my phone like I knew she would and I don't stop her.

"No bedtime," Bridget says then pouts. It's a truly impressive pout, one where she sticks out her bottom lip and flashes puppy dog eyes at me. With both my hands on the ottoman, I lean down and give her forehead a kiss. "I told you only one show. Come on now," I say then hold my hand out to her, standing up straight and Bridget follows my lead. "Time to brush our teeth."

"Night night, little miss."

"Night night, Raynay."

Even though Bridget sounds completely defeated, she doesn't fight bedtime. With the little yawn she gives me as her bare feet pad on the floor, I know she'll be out like a light in only a few minutes.

It's only when she's tucked in with her night light on and the door open an inch, just how she likes it, that I head back to the living room. Brushing my hair out of my face, I let my cheeks puff out with an exaggerated sigh.

"So what is the plan?" I ask Renee, feeling that nervous pitter-patter in my chest.

It's late, the night is dark and the salty breeze is now a little too chilly for the window to be cracked, so I close it. Renee hasn't answered, so I turn around to face her and lift a brow as I say, "How can I tell him?"

Renee stretches out her legs and rests her head on the back of the chair before grinning like a fool and holding up my phone. "I don't know but I like kissing you," she jokes and then laughs, and I can't help but smile.

And to toss a pillow at her smiling face.

"You're no help."

Chapter 18

Brody

The smell of wood stain is overwhelming. It engulfs me as I lay down another sample of granite on the plywood that will be the bar top.

"I still like the steel best," Griffin calls out from across the room. Of course he has his laptop open, his feet propped up while I do the manual labor.

A few of the painters look his way, probably wondering what the hell he's talking about and if it relates to them. Griffin's gaze never leaves the documents on the screen and everyone goes about their business.

There are at least a dozen guys in this place day in and day out. Construction is practically finished with the exception of some of the plumbing that needs updating and the same goes for the wiring.

It's eating up a good chunk of the money I set aside for this part of our business. I love the brewery, but it better pay me back. Between the steel countertop and the gray slab of marble with the waterfall edge, there's no doubt we'd save money on the steel that Griffin keeps going on about.

"You like the steel look or you like the price tag?" I call out to where he's seated in the booth and that gets his attention.

"If I say both, will you know I'm lying?" he asks and a huff of a laugh leaves me.

The steel may be economical, but the vision in my head, the shared dream of this bar … it calls for a pricier aesthetic.

Exhaling and heading to the cooler, I decide we can look at the numbers again. We can push the online retail and the partnerships we have lined up. A little more time may not be so bad. It'll be better than opening a subpar bar.

With a beer in hand, the water beads dripping down to my wrist, I sit across from Griffin. I don't expect him to stop working when I ask him a question; he never stops working if that laptop is open.

"Who the hell is Robert Barnes?" My swig is short because of the look Griffin gives me. It's a cautious gaze behind his glasses.

"The guy we have a meeting with?"

"The guy who happens to be Magnolia's ex," I say, my response immediate and firm.

"That girl's gotten to you," is all he says and then he's back at it.

A moment passes and then another as I read through our texts.

She likes kissing me too. Just reading that sends a warmth through me. "Yeah, she's gotten to me," I admit to him and take another swig. This new batch is going to be a bestseller. Smooth with a hint of citrus. Not too bad on the calories. We created the batch for our female clientele and I would bet good money that this is the one the taste testers pick.

My mind isn't even on Magnolia anymore. I'm too consumed with all of the dollar signs and work I see when I take in each space of what will be our bar. Until Griffin asks, "I thought you didn't want to know?"

"What do you mean?" I don't like the way he asked that question and I'm sure he can tell that from my tone and the pinched expression marring my face.

"You said you didn't want to know the gossip and rumors and all that?" Even though his statement is somewhat accusatory, it's still voiced as a question.

The glass bottom of the brown bottle in my hand thuds on the plywood tabletop. "What do you know that I don't?" There's a stillness around us and I don't like it. "You said he's an ex, still harboring feelings. You said there was drama—"

"And you said you didn't care," Griffin butts in, closing the laptop and leaving the booth in favor of the cooler closer to the bar. "Which is good." His last statement catches me off guard. I even flinch, which only makes him continue.

"You talked about her nonstop years ago."

"I was just asking if you saw her after I left."

"Yeah, I remember. Your big dumb puppy dog pout wasn't fooling anyone." His sigh is full of frustration. "She's the one you wanted a chance with and now you're here; she's here. It's one hell of a coincidence."

"What is your point?"

"That you should go for her and give it your best shot. You're holding back and it's pissing me off."

"Well damn," I comment, genuinely shocked.

"I'm sorry, but I think she'd be good for you and I think you need to ... I don't know, bro. I don't know what you need but I'm pretty sure it involves her."

"So why are you yelling at me for thinking about her?"

"Because you don't want to know the details. The details matter."

My gaze follows him. "What if I change my mind? What if I want to know everything there is to know about her?" Adrenaline kicks in, forcing my pulse to race a little harder. I know Magnolia, although she's still Rose in my mind, is hiding something. She barely talks about herself when we're together, I have to pry every little detail out of her in between our heated kisses ...

"You know anything about her daughter?" I ask him. I

haven't met her and I don't know how to even go about bringing it up. "I've never dated someone with a kid. If I send Magnolia flowers, should I send a small bouquet for her kid too?" I was thinking about doing just that. And then I thought it might cross a line since she hasn't brought up meeting her. I don't want to ignore her, though. That seems ... dickish.

"What did she tell you?" Griffin asks, and it's surprising that he doesn't get back to work. A prick travels up the back of my neck at how serious he seems right now. From the stern expression to the way his hands are clasped in front of him.

"Her name's Bridget."

"She didn't tell you how old she is?" he asks and my pulse slows down just a tad when I shake my head. "She should be about three right now ... a little older than three. You said you and Magnolia hooked up about four years ago?" I let the words sink in, and then the reality hits me.

There's no fucking way. My next question comes out rough and I have to clear my throat to repeat it. "When's her birthday?"

"Do I really need to tell you for you to put the pieces together?" Griffin asks.

Oh fuck.

CHAPTER 19

MAGNOLIA

"This graph is not my favorite thing in the world right now." My comment is reserved for the soda can in my hand. I click, click and drop the link to it in the email, but I don't send it yet. Instead I lean back, have a sip of my soda and note the downward trend.

It's in direct correlation with the headline of Mandy's email: Why are sales down?

The prints and even originals have dropped in sales recently and she wants to know why and what to do moving forward. Typing out my answer, I refer to the graph. Specifically, the last time we had new material to share on social media and update on the ad listings. We've got to keep it fresh and new with the products we're promoting and the bottom line is, we haven't gotten in a new artist or line for over a month now, so it makes sense that sales have declined in the last week and a half.

I'm confident in the explanation, but still, I grimace reading my response. I finish the drink and set the empty aluminum can on the end table before typing away with an update on the upcoming gala.

It's all set. Everything is arranged. We could have an additional artist and drive someone new and upcoming for publicity.

Art never goes stale, but one thing is more important when it comes to marketing. Everyone loves the newest and even more than that ... a sale. Bring them in with the new, hook them with the sale.

Nerves run through me, wracking my body as I hit send. It's nearly nine and I've been working on this data analysis spreadsheet for five hours now. I'm so exhausted I could fall asleep right here. Between preschool, the list Mandy gave me to execute, and coming up with a solution to this very real problem, I have run myself into the ground this past week. More than that, I'm anxious that Mandy isn't going to agree or want to go with any of the new artists I recommended.

Rubbing my tired eyes with the heel of my palms, I remind myself I've done everything I can. That's all I can do.

Knock, knock. The knock at the door makes me hold my

breath as I quickly turn around to stare down the hall. My eyes are laser focused on Bridget's bedroom. As if I can see through the walls and know instantly if she woke up.

Shoot, shoot, shoot. I'm quick to set the laptop on the coffee table, nearly tossing it down to get to the door before whoever's there can knock again.

Who would come over this late at night? The question makes me feel more annoyed as I unlock the lock and pull open the door.

Until I see Brody standing there.

The anxiousness from work? Nonexistent.

The annoyance that someone would wake up Bridget? Dulled.

Guilt-ridden nerves spread through every inch of me as I wrap my robe tighter around myself and feel the salty night breeze shift my hair off my shoulders ... yup, that's what takes over. Guilt.

All because of the look in his eyes. There's a worry there, a knowing look. I can barely breathe as I swallow thickly. "Brody, you're here late."

My murmur is even and then, glancing behind me to check Bridget's door one last time, I step outside and gently close the door behind me.

The stars are out tonight, the moon too and its light filters through the leaves of the overgrown trees that line the park out front. "You couldn't call?"

My heart hammers, slowly but with precision at the sight of him. His black T-shirt is stretched across his broad shoulders, his striped shorts making him look like a model for some overpriced store at the mall a town over. But his hair is rumpled, and his expression lacking any charm, only hurt. His eyes tell me everything I need to know.

Still, I wait for him. "Bridget is sleeping... so," I say and don't bother finishing. The crickets from the park have made their presence known and it's just them and us out here on my porch.

"You have a daughter?"

"Yes ... I told you." Even to my own ears, it sounds like an excuse.

"Who's three?" he asks, and the light in his eyes dims.

"Yes," I answer and swallow a lump of spikes in my throat. The unspoken question surrounds us and it threatens to be spoken if I don't speak up myself: How could you not tell me?

"I don't know ... who the father is," I say and it hurts to admit the truth. Brody's sneakers smack down on the pavement as he turns his back to me. At first, I think he's leaving, and it kills something inside I wanted to protect, but he's only moved to sit on the porch step.

Tears leak from the corner of my eyes and I'm quick to brush them away, grateful he doesn't see. I dealt with this shame years ago; I don't want to go back to the girl I was back then.

"I was getting over my ex when we met at the bar."

"Robert." Brody says the name, clearly up to date.

"Yes," I say and slowly, very slowly, I join him on the porch, taking a seat next to him and using the railing to lower me down.

His shoulders are hunched and the crickets pipe up once again in our silence.

"How could you not tell me?" I knew he would ask, but I still wasn't prepared for how much it would hurt to hear him say it like an accusation.

"I left that week and I didn't find out for two more months …" I still remember that moment. Having nothing, having no one and then realizing I hadn't gotten my period since I'd been back. "I was shocked and I didn't have your number or—"

"You knew where I was staying," Brody cuts me off to insist, allowing both disappointment and anger to leak into the accusation.

"I didn't. I was drunk, Brody. I didn't even know your last name. I … was reckless and—" My throat tightens, explaining everything all over again. Feeling the shame and the remorse. I shouldn't feel those emotions about my baby girl. I hate that I'm back in that place I was years ago. Feeling just as alone and like the scarlet letter on my chest is burning brighter than it did back then.

I sniffle, fighting back the tears, knowing that this is what it was all leading to, and it's only then that Brody touches me. His large hand settles down on my thigh, half resting on the edge of my cotton nightgown and half on my bare skin. I'm grateful for the small bit of mercy and I'm quick to put my left hand over his. My right is busy brushing away the tears.

"Is she mine?"

"I don't know. If I knew for sure, I'd tell you—but I don't ..." A long moment passes of quiet and I pull my hand away, in case he wants his own back. "It doesn't matter because I'm not asking for anything if she is. I don't want to put that pressure on you."

His response comes with an edge when he says, "I have a right to know."

"I know," I say and my voice is just as defensive. "I know you do. But I thought I would never see you again." I swallow down the next words that beg to tumble out. The ones that explain how I prayed and wished on every star that he would come to my rescue years ago. Like how little girls wish for their Prince Charming to take care of all their problems. I hoped that he would magically find me. I could tell him everything and that he would love me at a time in my life when so many people hated me. That he would see I was pregnant and that he'd want to know and help me through it all. But all the prayers and wishes were only words whispered at night that sometimes helped me sleep. Come every morning, I was alone. Robert was there too, sometimes. But Brody? I learned to accept I would never see him again.

I settle on a simple truth when he pulls his hand away. "I wanted to tell you for months, but you weren't there to tell. So I just ... I just learned to accept that it was never going to happen. Years later, you show up out of nowhere and expect me to be able to tell you. I don't think you understand everything that it comes with. It's not so simple, Brody." I don't realize that I have officially lost it, the tears streaming and my nose running until I sniffle and recognize that I need a tissue.

I'm only vaguely aware that Brody stands up with me, his hand gracing the small of my back for a fraction of a second as I hurry inside. I leave the door open for him and from the hall half bath, I know he shut the door from the thud that echoes back here.

Bracing a hand on the counter on each side of the sink, I gather my courage, not knowing if he came inside or simply left.

I don't know which would be easier to take right now, because all I feel like doing is sagging into my bed and letting all of this out. Just to get it over with and move on.

With a gentle knock, the bathroom door creaks open and Brody stands behind me in the mirror. "You all right?" he asks and my shoulders hunch, my hands cover my face and I can only shake my head no.

I give myself a full second, maybe two, before reaching for the tissue box again only to find it empty and relying on toilet paper in its place. "I just need a moment and I'll tell you everything." My reddened eyes stare at his in the mirror as I say, "I promise. I'll tell you anything you want to know. I just need a moment."

CHAPTER 20

BRODY

"I keep telling myself, there's no way for you to know what I'm feeling right now and what I went through." Magnolia's face crumples as she adds in a strained voice, "But I wish you could. I wish you knew what this felt like and how much I wish everything was different. I've wished it for years.

"I never wanted to keep anything from you. I never wanted to hurt you. I was just hurting myself and it kept me ..." Her gaze drifts to the hallway every time her voice raises slightly. I don't miss it. Her little girl, possibly my little girl, is tucked away sleeping.

My hands are raised as I go to her, the distance disappearing as I wrap my arms around her small frame. She sags against my chest although she doesn't let her face touch my shirt. Instead her forearms are braced there.

I imagined this scene for hours before I came, ever since Griffin told me. He said he figured she was Robert's until the rumor mill started up and there were whispers that it was some guy she hooked up with in college who'd knocked her up.

For all I know, that little girl could be Robert's, my child, or someone else's. But she should have told me if there was even a chance that she was mine.

That's all I was thinking on the drive down here.

I didn't know I'd feel like this. I didn't know she'd break down like she is. "I don't want you to be upset," I whisper in her hair, rocking her slightly and running my hand up and down her back.

Magnolia doesn't say anything, but she does try to pull away and I don't want her to. I don't know a lot of things right now, but I know when she backs away and heads to the bathroom, I wish she didn't. I wish she'd lay her head against me and let her tears land wherever they land; I'd still hold her.

With nothing in my arms and feeling a weight on my chest, I plant myself down on her sofa. My elbows rest on my knees as I lean forward. It was one night years ago. A single night. My grandfather's voice jokes in the back of my head: It only takes once.

"There's a chance she's yours. And there's a chance she's not," Magnolia admits to me. "I didn't know how to tell you when she's ... she's my whole world and it feels like no matter what I do, it comes back on her." It takes great effort on her part to keep the fresh tears back and I hate to see her like this.

I don't know how to make things right, but I want to.

My mind races with every possible thought until she sits down beside me. Leaving space between us, far too much space. With my chin propped up on my closed fist, I peek at her.

Her red-rimmed eyes barely glance back. Everything makes sense now. Every little detail all lining up. I know I'm not feeling what she's feeling, but damn it hurts. It's too much.

"Dahlia, you look prettier when you smile," I joke with her and her expression falters a moment until she sees me smile. Rose. Magnolia. It doesn't matter what she calls herself.

"Dahlia now?" A hint of a smile touches her flushed face.

"They're beautiful flowers," I whisper back with a smirk. "Come here," I say, giving her the small command, leaning back and gesturing with my hand. She's slow to fold herself into my arms but she does. This time her cheek rests against my chest and her hand lays right in the center of it.

"Which one is a dahlia?" she asks me and my chest vibrates with a chuckle, stirring her.

"I have no idea, to be honest." She smiles broader and I feel it. My smile widens too when she readjusts, sneaking closer to me until her leg is pressed against mine and my arm fully wraps around her back. "It's the first flower name that came to me after Rose and Magnolia," I say.

There's a small bit of peace and stillness that rests between us. Her guard is still up when she tells me, "I really, really like you, but I mean it when I say she's my whole world and that I don't know what to do to protect her from this ..."

All I can think is that this town is going to talk and judge. The animosity Magnolia got when her father screwed over this town is what she's afraid of. Not the part directed at her, but in the way they'll look at and talk about her daughter.

It's all too heavy and all too much.

I confess the only thing I can think to admit. "I want to kiss you."

She peeks up at me, her tired eyes glossy again. "Even still?" she asks. The pain and insecurity are raw and vibrant in her doe eyes.

"Even more seeing you like this."

With my hand cupping her chin, I press my lips to hers, silencing all of that uncertainty.

She's quick to deepen it and her slender fingers wrap around the back of my neck. What was peaceful turns hot in an instant.

I nip her bottom lip and peek down at her, her eyes still closed when I kiss her again. My tongue sweeps across the seam of her lips and she parts them for me, granting me entrance.

I'm hard and in need and there's no way she isn't in need too. The sofa protests with a groan as I lay her down, never taking my lips off hers. My hands roam up her nightgown and it's only then that she breaks our kiss, breathing heavily and whispering my name like a plea.

Please don't deny me. For the love of all things holy, please don't deny me.

"We have to be quiet," is the only warning she gives me and I devour those sweet lips of hers and rush to undress us both.

Her hand is hot and full of the same need every inch of her is giving me as she slips her fingers up my shirt. With the scratch of her nails, the strokes of her tongue against mine and the gentle moaning, her desire and need meet my own.

It's a cloud of lust and longing that unveils itself around us in the dark night in her living room. Her sofa groans as she lays down and I meet every inch of her movements with mine. Skin on skin, heat on heat, there's nothing between us, nothing stopping us.

Raking my teeth up her neck I listen to the sweet gasp of pleasure that spills from her lips. Slipping my hand between her legs, I find her ready.

With the tip of my finger I gently play with her clit, loving how she writhes under me.

She begs and pleads, the arch of her foot pressed against my ass to push me closer to her.

"Brody, I want you," she murmurs with lust laying over every word.

The spark in her eyes, the heavy rise and fall of her chest, and my name on her lips fuels me to let go of everything and all sense, and take her like I've wanted to.

With a swift movement, I thrust all of myself into her in a single movement. Her eyes widen, her bottom lip drops and her nails dig into my skin. She's tight, so fucking tight.

Pain and pleasure swirl in her doe gaze and I wait for her body to relax, planting small kisses along her jawline. I take my time with them and when she's finally able to breathe, I slow my motions and rock into her, stretching out her pleasure and loving how every time I fill her, she whimpers with lust.

"Brody." Her whispers urge me to never let a moment pass where I'm not concerned with what she needs and how right this feels between us.

It's slow and steady until she finds her release and then the selfish part of me takes over, lifting her left leg, pinning her down and fucking her into the cushion as she bites down on my shoulder to muffle her screams of pleasure.

With the window still cracked, a soft breeze blows in the room, making Magnolia shiver. The thin chenille throw barely covers her, let alone the two of us, so I bend down to pick up my shorts.

Her wide eyes meet mine and I know she's wondering if I'm leaving. "Just closing the window." She stays where she is, neither of us saying a word as the window shuts with a creak.

I imagine I'm not welcome to stay, so I won't ask for that. All I can imagine is a sweet little three-year-old, waking up to see a strange man she's never met before.

All that emotion stirs in my chest again. Our moment of distraction over.

She lifts her head as I sit back down so she can rest it in my lap. Still quiet.

"Did Robert take a paternity test?" I dare to ask. I pet her hair, hoping the touching and staying calm will let her know I'm not mad and I'm not going anywhere. Her tongue darts out to wet her still swollen lips and she answers, "No. He didn't."

It's quiet for a long moment. All I do is nod in response until I gather the courage to ask her, "Can I meet her?"

Keeping the throw wrapped tight around her to cover herself, Magnolia sits up and leaves me, making a beeline for a photograph hung on the wall. She doesn't hesitate to take it down.

Without a word she stands in front of me, offering the black wood frame.

"So many curls," I say and rack my brain as I take in every feature. I don't think any of my family has curls like that.

"From my family," Magnolia says and tucks her hair behind her ear. "If my hair was shorter, I'd still have curls." Although the air is tenser, she takes a seat beside me. "She looks a lot like I did when I was younger.

I note her eyes the most. The shape is all Magnolia, but they're pale blue. So pale. Robert's are like that and I'm surprised how much that hurts to realize. I don't know if she is mine or his. Not by looking at a photo.

Handing the frame back I say, "She's beautiful, like you."

With a simper she takes the photo back and stands, the cotton nightgown falling just beneath her ass as she strides across the living room to place the frame where it belongs. Everything just so, in a modest home, obviously laid out for a family.

It's in this moment I realize I'm in the home of a woman who has struggled on her own, yet she still smiles. She's been alone in a world that can be brutal, especially in a town like this, and worst of all, with every action she takes there's a small voice reminding her that it all comes down on her daughter. Just like her father's actions came down on her.

And who am I to stand next to a woman like her? High risk, high reward, never sit still, never look back—has been my motto for years. The only time I ever looked back was to think about her and that one night, because I wanted more of her but she wasn't there where I thought she'd be.

It's not just the two of us. The gentle creak of a toy box is opened and Magnolia busies herself putting away a few stray items. This late at night, she's still going and all I can think is that I wasn't prepared for this, but then again, neither was she.

CHAPTER 21

MAGNOLIA

I can still feel him. He left me sore; it's the good kind, though. The morning light filters in through the kitchen and without much up and about at this hour, the sound of his car engine revving to life is nearly as loud as the coffee machine.

The smell of the fresh brew surrounds me and I inhale deeply, grateful that we woke up before Bridget and that Brody was just fine sneaking out this early in the morning.

I suppose this is a different kind of walk of shame than the one I took four years ago.

My head is killing me and even the first sip of coffee doesn't help. Crying that hard will do it, I suppose. Although if anyone asks, I'll tell them it's allergies. After all, the seasons are changing.

My phone pings from where it's plugged in on the kitchen counter and after rinsing the spoon I used to stir in the creamer, I read my friend Autumn's text about a playdate this weekend.

Playdate at the library? It's 9 am on Saturday.

There's a reading group where the kids play in their section and then Mrs. Harding reads classics to them while they sit cross-legged.

Yes, perfect. I'll see you there.

Bridget loves Henry and Chase. The three of them are as thick as thieves although they're two years older than her.

I stare at my phone, wondering who I can talk to about the one thing that's been on my mind since I laid eyes on Brody. A paternity test. I don't know a soul who's ever needed one in this town ... I don't feel comfortable asking my doctor either. She's Robert's neighbor and I remember the look she gave me when I stared back at her in disbelief that I was pregnant.

There's no way in hell I'd ask that woman for a paternity test. Patient confidentiality my ass; you can read what that woman is thinking with every expression she makes. The hmms of confirmation and raised eyebrows add to silent conversations I know she has.

I'm certain I can buy one online. You can get anything and everything online nowadays. Away from prying eyes.

Glancing down, I realize my texts are opened up to the ones between Robert and me. The last few are innocent messages. Telling me he knows the gala will be amazing. That he's ordered specific champagne for the politicians he's invited to the event so he can rub elbows with them.

With a numbing prick in my hand, I can't text him that I'm going to get a test. The chill runs from the tip of my fingers all the way to my heart.

When I told him about the pregnancy years ago, he was happy. He was genuinely happy. Until I told him about Brody.

It's complicated is … such an underused statement.

Picking at my nails I decide I'll order the test, Brody will want to take it and that's all I need really. With the realization that I'll know definitively who the father is, I try to swallow but my throat is tight. Opening up the cabinet drawer, I take out the Advil, listening to the bottle rattle and take out three. I down them with my coffee before ordering the test on my phone once and for all.

I didn't ask Brody to stay last night, but I also didn't ask him to leave. And he stayed.

That is my plan in all of this, even if it feels like it's tearing me up on the inside. I won't ever ask a man to stay, but I can't imagine ever asking either of the two of them to leave.

"Mommy, are you okay?" Bridget's voice surprises me from behind and I'm quick to turn around and smile. Her little baby voice is full of worry until I boop her on her nose and tell her good morning.

"Mommy's allergies are acting up this morning," I say,

lying to her and scrunch my nose.

She makes a sniffling sound while pulling at the hem of her Paw Patrol pink nightgown and climbing onto her seat for breakfast.

With my back to her, I pull myself together and get out a bowl and Cheerios before she even has a chance to tell me she wants cereal for breakfast. I already know she does. My girl loves her milk.

Me with my coffee and her with her cereal, we sit at the table like we do every morning, but today is so much different.

"Mommy loves you more than anyone, you know that, right?" I ask her and she doesn't bother looking up as she slurps her milk and nods at the same time. I tell her, "More than anyone in the whole wide world, I love you the most."

CHAPTER 22

BRODY

Charlie's is never empty. That's one thing I have learned about this small town. And the two roast beef sandwiches I'm waiting on are one of the many reasons why. I don't know who Charlie is, but the restaurant in his name makes a damn good meal.

Even from the patio, I can faintly hear the sounds of power saws from down the street. That would be the granite counter being fitted for the bar tops. Griffin and I decided this morning that one thing is clear: we're not in competition with Charlie's. No sandwiches, salads and chef's specials that involve homemade bread.

We're going to offer a different menu, more pub-like and

less comfort food. We definitely need fried pickles. That's a given. I'm drawn back to the bar where I first met Magnolia. Something like that. That's what I want. And Griffin is easygoing enough to agree to it all. Although he pointed out if we don't get the legalities sorted out, it's going to be a BYOB situation for us, and no one goes into a pub expecting not to get a tall glass at the bar.

"Brody, right?" A masculine voice from behind me catches my attention. The afternoon breeze is cooler than it's been. Fall is slipping into the color of the trees lining the sidewalk too. Still, the suit jacket Robert wears seems … unnecessary. The T-shirt I'm wearing is just fine for this weather. Even if it is a little colder than it's been.

"Robert," I answer him back by speaking his name and hold out my hand. He's got a firm shake, one I can respect although I don't know what to think about him. Even though he's as tall as me, his build is slighter. His proper haircut and clean shave make him look slightly older too.

"Nice to formally meet you."

"I think we were supposed to meet the other day for business." I recall Griffin saying he was the one we were supposed to meet with for the alcohol license.

"Yes, that's right," Robert says, slipping his hands into his pockets. "Your new bar is the talk of the town." I almost question him further about it, but he adds, "Among other things."

"And what would those other things be?" I ask him,

knowing damn well he's referring to Magnolia. A slight movement to my right makes me glance back to see a to-go bag has been placed down beside me. Mary Sue, the young waitress who took my order, has already turned around, leaving the two of us to ourselves.

"I don't want to keep you from lunch," Robert says and my attention is turned back to him. His blue gaze meets mine with complete seriousness. "I just want to let you know she's a good girl and she doesn't need someone coming in and messing up her life."

"You speak for Magnolia?" My anger gets the best of me and it seeps into the question.

With a heavy sigh, he looks past me a moment and shakes his head. "She speaks for herself." He meets my gaze again and adds, "But that doesn't mean you shouldn't already know what I said is true."

"I'm not here to mess up anything."

"She already has someone. So back off."

I remain unbothered although my eyes narrow. "Sounds like you guys are a thing?"

"We are and I'm sure you know we are."

"See, that's confusing, though, because the town says you aren't. And Magnolia says she's single."

"I plan on changing that tonight," he says and nods his head like it's a done deal. "Maybe we kept it low key before, but I'm all in with Mags and everyone knows that."

"Doesn't seem like you," I tell him.

"I'm willing to leave with her, pick up and go." His confidence rises and I don't know why. Magnolia hasn't hinted that she wants to leave. It's been just the opposite. "Are you willing to do that? Change your life for her? Because I am."

The intensity of the conversation increases with every passing second. Until he clears his throat and glances past me to the three waitresses who are just behind us, setting a single table.

As if it isn't obvious they're listening. My annoyance couldn't be any greater.

"I sent the paperwork over to your company's email. Congratulations on your bar." Robert's regards come with a nod and he moves to turn his back to me.

"You signed it?" I'm not going to lie, a piece of me thought he wouldn't, just to keep me out of town and away from Magnolia. Everything about this guy throws me off.

"Yeah, it's all signed. I think I may be long gone by the time it opens, though. And just so you know, I plan on taking Magnolia with me."

Chapter 23

Magnolia

"I'm relieved he's the one who messaged, though," I say to Renee, who is seated on the other side of my kitchen island. Slipping in my favorite earrings, I add, "I needed to message him anyway," I lower my voice so Bridget can't hear, "about the test."

"That's good dinner conversation," she jokes flatly and then calls out, "What do you want for dinner, Bridge? Scagetti?" She mimics the way Bridget says spaghetti and the two of them clap when my little girl shrieks with joy.

"But what's he want to talk about?"

"He didn't say. I would think it's a new position maybe?" He's always kept me up to date whenever something's changed for him. When he bought a house, when he transferred departments. Every step of the way, he's kept me informed. "Something must've changed," I say and slip on my heels.

"Yeah ... it has nothing to do with Romeo showing up?"

"I told you." With my voice lowered I remind her, "I told him about Brody already."

"Yes, you told me. You told me he understood and I told you politicians are bred to be liars." She rolls her eyes just like she did last time.

"Well, whatever it is," I tell her, picking up my car keys, "I'll spill the beans when I get home. Promise."

"Enjoy your fancy dinner," she calls out after me, "I'm going to enjoy my fine dining with my favorite little girl in the whole wide world."

I have to smile as I kiss the top of Bridget's head, who's hard at work scribbling in her coloring book. "Love you, my little miss."

She's too invested in the red and blue swirls so I head out with a wave and say thanks again to Renee.

The drive there, I can only think about two things: how I forgot my jacket so it's going to be chilly with only this sleeveless cotton dress on, but mostly, how the last time I was at Morgan's I was having an official first date with Brody.

Clicking the radio off, I let the turmoil eat me up. I'm with Brody now. I'm not a girl who sleeps around and even though Brody didn't say anything to make it official, I am not doing anything with Robert while I'm seeing another man.

As I hit every red light on the way there, I groan. Feels like a sign this conversation isn't going to go oh so well.

That's the thing with Robert, though, I can have any conversation I need with him. I always have.

We should have done this years ago. It's all I can think as I walk into the restaurant and make my way to where Robert's sitting. He stands like a gentleman and pulls out my chair.

"You forgot your jacket?" he asks with an asymmetric grin. Rubbing my arms, I scrunch my nose and tell him, "I'll warm up."

When he politely pushes in my chair, I thank him and then the waiter who's already beside me with a menu.

My nerves rattle, but even as I order a drink, I keep thinking we should have done this years ago. "We should have had a paternity test years ago." My hushed comment slips out the second the waiter has let us be.

The ease and peace I feel with the decision today is not at all reflected in Robert's surprised eyes. Regret instantly consumes me.

With a glass of wine to help me settle, I take a sip of ice water as he reaches for his tumbler of whiskey.

"A paternity test?" he asks and the thud of the glass on the table matches the thud in my chest.

"You don't think so?" I whisper the question and his head shakes silently as the waiter sets my glass of wine down.

"Thank you," I manage to get out with a small smile, even though Robert's lips are pressed in a thin line.

"It's not that I want anything … legally."

"It's not that, Mags." The words rush out of him and worry plays across his handsome features. With a hand running down his face he lets out a rush of air and adds, "This is not what I wanted to talk about tonight."

"I'm sorry." That guilt in the pit of my stomach climbs up higher.

"Don't be; it's all right," he tells me and lays his hand out on the table, palm up, coaxing me to take it. I can only stare at his outstretched hand in disbelief. We've had plenty of dinners together in public. And I've held his hand privately many a time. But … public affection? PDA or whatever it's called? There's an unspoken rule between us that we don't cross that line.

Pulling his hand back, he continues, his cadence easy. "If that's what you want to do."

"You don't want to know?" I ask him with earnest.

Robert hesitates and it's then that I see how tired he looks. The darkness under his eyes and how his normally cleanly shaved jaw shows more than a five o'clock shadow. "Is everything okay?" I ask and the waiter interrupts the moment, laying down fresh bread and oil on the table.

Once he's gone, Robert smiles at me. A soft smile that I know well. "I didn't know you were ready for more," he says and there's a sadness in his tone that's unlike him.

Shifting in my seat, I pull both hands into my lap. "I don't know what to say," I tell him, my appetite vanishing.

"I would wait forever for you," he starts and I cut him off.

"You broke up with me," I remind him.

"And then you needed me and I went right back to you," he tells me like that's what happened.

"It wasn't the same." He knows that. It's not like he took me back. It's not like I wanted him back either. "My whole life fell apart and you were there for me, but as a friend."

"I—I," his frustration shows but it's not directed at me. With his eyes closed, his next words are pleading. "Do you think I have what we have with all of my friends?" His pale blue eyes beg me as he adds, "Really, Mags? I didn't know you were ready or that you wanted more."

My silence is met with a plea from him. "I deserve a chance."

He may have been surprised by the paternity test, but not as surprised as I am sitting here.

"That's what this dinner is?" I ask him and as I cross my legs, I can still feel Brody from last night. I've never felt like a whore before. The town whispered that word and slut when they found out I was pregnant and there wasn't a single moment I felt like it was deserved. But sitting here now, having this conversation ... I truly think less of myself.

"We can leave, Mags. We can go up north, wherever you want."

"What?"

"It's more liberal," he tells me and his tone adds in that he's got a whole speech prepared for me.

"I can't even wrap my head around what you're saying right now. You want to move? Not just across town but away from here?"

"Don't you? You wanted to when we were young. Under our angel oak tree."

My eyes prick with tears remembering that old tree that sits in the center of town and the promises we made together. "We were kids and didn't know any better."

"Mags, you name a place, I'll go with you. We'll start fresh. Me, you, and Bridget?"

"Bridget may not—"

"I don't care if I'm not her father." Robert's voice is louder than intended and I know other people may have heard. He doesn't bother to look around us, but he does take in a steadying breath. "I'll do the test if you want to know, but I don't care about that. I care that I've been there for her every step of the way when I could. You did it all and I'm not trying to take away from that, but I did everything you wanted."

My mind plays the reel back, wondering what the hell I've been thinking all these years.

"I didn't mean to use you." I'm careful and slow with my words, wondering if I took advantage of him. A voice in the back of my head tells me I did. Sitting here now with him, how could I not have known how he feels?

"You didn't take advantage of me. It's my fault," he says then takes in another deep breath followed by another swig of his whiskey. "I never asked the right questions or else I would have known you were ready."

"Ready?"

"For a relationship," he answers and his strong hand that's been over every inch of my body lays out on the table again.

"Robert ..." I'm stunned, truly. He's saying all the right things, but ... why now?

"I want to make it official. I want to move up north and start fresh. I want it all with you, Mags. With you and Bridget."

"I slept with him." The confession slips out unbidden.

My gaze never leaves Robert's as I choke out, "Last night. I told him he might be Bridget's father and slept with him."

Feeling sick to my stomach, I let the silence settle between us.

"Are you ready to order?" the waiter asks and Robert offers the man the semblance of a polite smile and orders for both of us. He orders my favorite and exactly what I would have ordered myself. Because he already knows. He knows everything about me.

The air of confidence around him dissipates the moment

the waiter leaves. "You slept with him?"

"Yes," I say with a calm demeanor even though it eats me up inside. It shouldn't. I don't owe Robert an explanation, but I give it to him anyway. "I really like him."

"But you don't love him," he offers.

I can never repay him for the grace he gives me. There's no hostility, nothing but a simple question about love. My heart shatters for us when I realize that truth.

"No, I don't know him enough to love him like that."

Robert nods, his eyes glistening and holding a faint tinge of red, but he doesn't speak. He doesn't say anything at all although he does finish his drink.

I suppose I can't blame him.

"Say something, please." I hate the silence between us and the tense air. I never wanted this. I didn't think it would be like this.

"What do you want me to say, Mags?" He's obviously upset and my heart aches with his. Why does it feel like a breakup? I never wanted to feel this way with him. In all our highs and lows, I've only ever felt this way once and I can't go back to that night again. He tells me with all sincerity, "I still love you."

"I love you too." I'll always love him. He knows that. I know he does.

His response is immediate and resolute. "Then don't see him again."

"I can't just ignore him, Robert—" He cuts me off before

I can explain myself. My head is a whirlwind of thoughts and questions. My heart races with uncertainty but also hope. Hope that's long since been dormant but is now being stirred with low flames.

"You gave him a chance, Mags," he says and lays his hand on the table again. Because of the hurt in his gaze, I reach out this time, letting him hold me and I'm holding him just the same. "Don't I deserve a chance too?" he whispers and then he adds, much stronger, much more confident, "What if I asked you to marry me?"

About the Author

Thank you so much for reading my romances. I'm just a stay at home Mom and an avid reader turned Author and I couldn't be happier.

I hope you love my books as much as I do!

More by Willow Winters
www.willowwinterswrites.com/books